SHORT FEATHER

LARRY LOUDERMILK

SHORT FEATHER

The Pain of Memory / The Joy of Remembering

TATE PUBLISHING
AND ENTERPRISES, LLC

Short Feather
Copyright © 2016 by Larry Loudermilk. All rights reserved.

No part of this publication may be reproduced, stored in a retrieval system or transmitted in any way by any means, electronic, mechanical, photocopy, recording or otherwise without the prior permission of the author except as provided by USA copyright law.

This novel is a work of fiction. Names, descriptions, entities, and incidents included in the story are products of the author's imagination. Any resemblance to actual persons, events, and entities is entirely coincidental.

The opinions expressed by the author are not necessarily those of Tate Publishing, LLC.

Published by Tate Publishing & Enterprises, LLC
127 E. Trade Center Terrace | Mustang, Oklahoma 73064 USA
1.888.361.9473 | www.tatepublishing.com

Tate Publishing is committed to excellence in the publishing industry. The company reflects the philosophy established by the founders, based on Psalm 68:11,

"*The Lord gave the word and great was the company of those who published it.*"

Book design copyright © 2016 by Tate Publishing, LLC. All rights reserved.
Cover design by Dante Rey Redido
Interior design by Jomar Ouano

Published in the United States of America

ISBN: 978-1-68097-705-9
Fiction / Native American & Aboriginal
16.08.26

But I say unto you, Love your enemies, bless them that curse you, do good to them that hate you, and pray for them which despitefully use you, and persecute you; That ye may be the children of your Father which is in heaven: for he maketh his sun to rise on the evil and on the good, and sendeth rain on the just and on the unjust.

—Matthew 5:44-45 (KJV)

Short Feather is dedicated to the many people who have chosen love over hate, in spite of being hated, used, abused, and persecuted.

The families and friends of those who were killed or wounded on June 17, 2015, at the Emanuel African Methodist Episcopal Church, Charleston, South Carolina, have set an example for all of us. We are both humbled and inspired by your love and strength of character.

Acknowledgments

Mom—for your encouragement and support.

Jane—my wonderful granddaughter, for listening to me read *Short Feather* and showing such great enthusiasm.

Bonnie, Anita, and Nancy—for being early readers of the manuscript. Your encouragement, support, and input have been priceless.

Nitanna Taylor—for reading the manuscript to make sure there was nothing that would offend Native Americans. This was very important to me.

Joyce—for being the love of my life (and a great proofreader).

Main Characters in 1966

The following are given in order of appearance. Brackets indicate the Indian name given by Short Feather.

Rudy Drake—Friend of Lee and Short Feather [Chero]
Short Feather—One-hundred-ten-year-old Cheyenne Indian
Lee Grant—Friend of Rudy Drake [White Tears]
Juanita Trujio—Short Feather's housekeeper [Buffalo Tail]
Jose Trujio—Juanita's brother
Maria Trujio—Jose's wife
Anna Trujio—Baby daughter of Jose and Maria
Dr. Jacob Bronson—Medical doctor [Healing Breeze]
Allison Bronson—Wife of Dr. Bronson [Warm Breeze]
Clara Lee Bronson—Baby daughter of Jacob and Allison [Breeze]
Snake / Henry Ott—Biker [Farting Horse]
Hugo / Hugh Westgate—Biker
Charles Ridley—Neighbor of Short Feather [Man of the Great Spirit / Charley]
Edward Conrad—Great-grandson of Short Feather [Tornado]
Miss Jane Goodyear—Nurse [Sunshine Woman]
Dr. Abigail Cook—Orthopedic surgeon, sister of Dr. Bronson [Bone Mender]
Mrs. Rhonda Watson—Neighbor of Short Feather [Grace]
Oskar—Mrs. Watson's miniature schnauzer
Mrs. Gunderson—Nurse [Nikita]

Main Characters in Short Feather's Stories (1864-1888)

The following are given in order of appearance.

Laughing Wolf—Short Feather's father
Buffalo Woman—Short Feather's mother
Peppermint—Short Feather's sister
Silas Soule—Army captain (real historical person)
Snow Flower (Snow)—Cheyenne interpreter
Maggie Lawson—White woman in Kansas
Thunderstorm (Storm)—Cheyenne Dog Soldier and brother of Snow Flower
Sunrise—Daughter of Snow Flower
Rain Catcher—Cheyenne boy found by Short Feather and Storm; son of Sage Woman
Sage Woman—Cheyenne widow and mother of Rain Catcher
Yellow Hawk—Cheyenne Dog Soldier
Little Hawk—Cheyenne Dog Soldier and brother of Yellow Hawk
Sgt. Jim Worthington—Soldier in Seventh Cavalry
Willow—Wife of Short Feather
Bright Star (Bridget)—Mother of Willow and Blue Sky
Blue Sky—Wife of Little Hawk and sister of Willow
Sky Hawk—Son of Little Hawk and Blue Sky
River—Daughter of Little Hawk and Blue Sky
Son of the Wind—Father of Willow and Blue Sky

Aspen—Daughter or Short Feather and Willow
John and Ruth Gale—Trading post proprietors
Stephen Aloysius Gregory (Buckskin)—Mountain man
William Ward III—Businessman from the East Coast

1

"Remembering the past helps us to understand the future."

—Short Feather

1966

The apartment building was one of those two-story stucco affairs in Pomona, California. It was nice but kind of dingy, with faded red doors and one window to the left of each door. Rudy walked up to number 7 and rang the doorbell.

The door opened, and a tall old bent Cheyenne Indian stood there looking at Rudy and Lee. The features of his long sharp dark-brown face were deeply lined. He was not happy to see them. There was a feather hanging down from his long gray hair, and he was leaning on two canes. He was wearing Snoopy pajama bottoms with a white T-shirt and old moccasins.

"Why do you bring this white man to my lodge, Chero?" asked the Indian. "I do not let them into my home, and you know this."

Rudy said, "Short Feather, this is Lee. We work together at the phone company, and—"

Short Feather held up his hand to stop Rudy from speaking. A cane hung between his thumb and index finger. He looked at Lee for a long time, starting at his shoes and, eventually, directly into his eyes. He turned to walk back into his apartment, his moccasins flopping with each small step.

"Bring him in, Chero," said Short Feather, "and close the door behind you."

Two Weeks Earlier

Rudy came into the lunchroom, got a cup of coffee, and sat across the table from Lee. "I see you have the manuscript. Did you read it?"

Lee looked at the folder he had in front of him. "Yes, I did. Actually, I read it twice. I find this to be a disturbing story. It says it was told to Sara Drake by an Indian named Standing Elk. Is Sara your wife?"

"Yes, Sara is my wife. She spent many days with Standing Elk and wrote down his story. He would only speak to her because she is a full-blood Cheyenne. He did not want to see me, and I am half-Cherokee. Standing Elk died shortly after telling his story to Sara."

Rudy went on. "I have worked here for ten years now and have offered this manuscript to many coworkers. You are the first to have read it all the way through, and you say you read it twice? Most either don't take it or say they are not interested and give it back."

"It is difficult to understand," said Lee, "and I was not always sure what I was reading. I knew about Custer and the Battle of the Little Bighorn—we were taught about that in school—but I had never heard of Sand Creek or Wounded Knee."

"Sara wrote down everything Standing Elk said and the way he said it. He was not good with English, and sometimes she had to ask others of his tribe to explain what he was saying." Rudy paused and looked at his hands. "Not many white people have heard of Sand Creek and Wounded Knee."

Break time ended, and they went back to work.

At lunch, Rudy asked, "Okay, Lee, what do you think?"

"I have always felt that the Indians were treated badly, but I did not know how badly," said Lee. "And I did a little research. It amazes me that the US government broke almost every promise and treaty. It is no wonder that Standing Elk was bitter."

Rudy was thoughtful for a minute. "Lee, would you like to meet a friend of mine? He is one hundred and ten years old, and a full-blood Cheyenne Indian. He may not talk to you, and probably will not let you enter his home. He lost most of his family at the Battle of the Washita in 1868 when he was twelve years old."

"It would be an honor to meet him. Should I bring a gift?" asked Lee.

"No, he would not respond well to a gift, and he may just turn us away. I'll arrange a time. Also, you need to know that he will call me Chero. His name is Short Feather, and he gives an Indian name to everyone that he likes. He picked Chero for me because I am half-Cherokee. And please, if he does agree to speak with us, do not say anything unless he speaks to you first."

Back at Short Feather's Apartment

Lee and Rudy followed Short Feather into his apartment, where he sat down in a large chair that was covered with a blanket. There was an old sofa, and Short Feather motioned for Lee and Rudy to sit.

The room was small and very clean with two full bookcases and more books neatly stacked on the floor. Lee was surprised to see an open Bible on a small table next to Short Feather's chair.

"Chero, tell me about this white man, Lee," said Short Feather.

"We work together at the phone company," Rudy answered. "He is a good worker, and we have become friends. I asked him to read Standing Elk's story. He read it twice and did some research."

Short Feather sighed. "I have often wondered why you do that, Chero. White people either don't know about what was done to the Indians or they don't care. Usually both."

Lee was becoming uncomfortable with them talking like he was not there but said nothing, remembering Rudy's instructions.

"What makes this white man, Lee, different?" asked Short Feather.

"I'm not sure," said Rudy. "It is a feeling I have based on things he has said and questions he has asked."

Short Feather again spoke only to Rudy. "I have similar feelings about this white man, and I have yet to hear him speak. He has the same eyes as a white man I met briefly many years ago. That white man had a good spirit. I have met few others that I could say that about. You have a good spirit, Chero, as you should, since you are half-Indian. What did this Lee say about Standing Elk?"

Rudy replied, "He said he could understand why Standing Elk was bitter toward white men."

Short Feather turned toward Lee and again looked directly into his eyes. "*Bitter* is an interesting word to describe Standing Elk's feelings, Lee. I would say *intense hatred* would be more appropriate. Standing Elk did not tell Chero's wife what had happened to his wife and children."

Pausing for a moment, Short Feather continued speaking slowly, and with great intensity. "Badly wounded and thought to be dead, Standing Elk witnessed white men murder his children. He then saw what the white men did to his wife before and after they killed her."

Tears started to fall from Lee's eyes.

"I will call you White Tears," said Short Feather. "You have a good spirit and remind me of Silas Soule. I only met him once when I was eight years old. Do you know who he was?"

"Yes, I do," said Lee. "He was a captain in the US Army and was at Sand Creek, but refused to take part in the murders. He also would not let the troops in his command take part. He later testified to what Colonel Chivington and his men had done."

"You are correct," said Short Feather. "And he was killed a few months later. Except for him and a few others, the white world may have never known the truth of Sand Creek."

"Sir, why did he not try to stop the massacre?" asked Lee.

"Those were difficult and confusing times. I believe that he did all that he could." Short Feather closed his eyes and became very quiet.

Rudy looked at Lee and put a finger to his lips. They sat quietly for about ten minutes.

Then Short Feather opened his eyes and said, "Please forgive my rudeness, I needed to go to a better place. Memories of those times are hard and painful. I do not speak of them often."

There was a knock at the door, and a pretty petite young Mexican woman walked in, carrying a bucket with cleaning supplies. She had beautiful shiny black hair, braided and reaching halfway down her back. At five feet four, to say she was well proportioned would be an understatement.

Lee stood, and Rudy followed his example. She stopped and looked at Short Feather with her head cocked to the side.

"Juanita, this is White Tears, and you know Chero," Short Feather said. He looked at the men. "This is Juanita, my little Mexican girlfriend. I think she wants to marry me."

Juanita laughed and said with a beautiful accent, "Ha, you are much too feisty and stubborn for me, you old Indian."

Juanita was twenty-two years old and had been cleaning for Short Feather for three years. They were close, and loved to tease and pick on each other.

She kissed Short Feather on the forehead. "How are you, my love? I worry about you."

"I think I am doing quite well for a one-hundred-and-ten-year-old human being, thank you," Short Feather answered.

"I am worried about your eyesight," said Juanita. "Did you know there is a white man standing in your living room?"

"I have given him a name, White Tears, and I believe we are becoming friends."

"God be praised," said Juanita. "I would never have believed it."

"He has a good spirit and seems to care about Indians. Judging by the way he stood when you came in, he cares about others as well. I may have to change his name to White Enigma."

Lee reached out to shake Juanita's hand. "It is a pleasure to meet you."

"Gracias, and please sit down. I need to do my cleaning." Juanita turned to go, but stopped. "And thanks for standing when I came in. That does not happen often. I was going to wait for the Indian to stand, but I don't have all day."

She kissed Short Feather again and went to clean the kitchen. Short Feather turned to watch her walk away, and then noticed that Lee was watching also.

"Be careful, White Tears, it is easy to fall in love with Juanita."

"I heard that, old man," Juanita said from the kitchen. "Now behave yourself. You know my heart belongs only to you."

2

> "History is told or written by human beings. The truth is elusive."
>
> —Short Feather

Short Feather got up and went into the bathroom.

Juanita came back to the living room. "Rudy, I don't understand. Do you think he is okay? I have never seen him let a white man into his home."

"It surprised me too," said Rudy. "But he does have what I would call biblical discernment, and he said Lee reminds him of Silas Soule."

"You must be very special, White Tears, and, Lee, is your real name?" asked Juanita.

"Lee Grant," said Lee. "Ironic, isn't it?"

"I think I'll just call you White Tears," said Juanita with a beautiful smile.

"Tell me, Juanita, if Short Feather gives a name to those he likes, why does he still call you Juanita?" asked Lee.

"That is quite simple. I told him that if he ever called me by the name he gave me, he would have to find another housekeeper."

"What name did he give you?"

Juanita did not answer, and went to the bathroom door. "Are you okay, old man?"

From the bathroom came, "I learned how to do this a long time ago and have had plenty of practice, but thanks for asking."

The toilet flushed.

"I love that old Indian," whispered Juanita as she went to the kitchen.

Short Feather came back to his chair. "One thing I really appreciate about the white man is indoor plumbing. Now, White Tears, what do you want to know about me? Ask me a question."

"I have many questions, but I will start with two," said Lee. "What name did you give to Juanita and how did you get your name?"

"I will answer the second question first. My father, Laughing Wolf, was a brave warrior and a skilled hunter, but he was also mischievous and had quite a sense of humor. My mother had no sense of humor at all, which gave rise to some interesting circumstances. I was an unusually large baby, and as I grew, I was always taller and huskier than the other children. Mother often complained about my weight and size, saying that I almost killed her in childbirth. Father named me Short Feather because I was tall and heavy. It was his attempt at sarcasm, and really annoyed my mother. She wanted to call me Almost Killed His Mother."

"What was your mother's name?" asked Lee.

"She was called Buffalo Woman, Hotoa Hehe, because she could skin and butcher a buffalo faster and better than any other in the tribe. She was strong and good with a knife."

Lee looked confused. "She could not have been called that as a child."

"She was called Nahtona, My Daughter, until she was fifteen," said Short Feather. He became thoughtful. "I did ask her once why she always complained about my birth. She looked at me with her usual disgusted no-nonsense look and said, 'Swallow a live buffalo calf and pass it from your body still alive. Then you will know what giving birth to you was like.' She walked away muttering to herself. I was sorry I had asked. The thought still haunts me."

"I'm sorry you told us," said Rudy. "I don't think I will ever get that vision out of my mind."

"I believe in sharing," said Short Feather, smiling.

"What about Juanita? What did you name her?" asked Lee.

"Don't you dare, old man," said Juanita as she came from the kitchen. "I really do not understand why you pay me to come and clean. There is always so little to do. For an old man, you certainly keep a clean apartment, so why am I here?"

"You bring sunshine to my home," said Short Feather.

Juanita kissed him on the forehead again and went to check the bathroom.

"I named her Hotoa Heva'se," Short Feather said to Lee.

"Buffalo Tail?" questioned Rudy.

"Now all three of you are in trouble," said Juanita from the bathroom.

Lee looked at Short Feather and said, "Sir, may I ask another question, a personal question?"

Short Feather licked his lips. "Chero, please get a pitcher of water and glasses. I am very thirsty. White Tears, you may ask as many questions as you would like, but I may not answer."

Lee waited for Rudy to return with the water. "Please do not be offended, but I have known elderly people much younger than you. Many are confused easily and have a hard time remembering yesterday, much less ten years ago. Your mind appears to be clear and sharp, and you remember a man's eyes from one hundred and two years ago. How do you explain this?"

Short Feather took a drink of water. "Do you pray, White Tears?"

"Yes, I do," Lee answered. "And I believe that God hears my prayers."

"As do I," said Short Feather. "But you must be careful. Sometimes, the Great Spirit gives you exactly what you ask. In my time on this earth, I have seen many terrible things and have witnessed much injustice. I asked the Great Spirit to help me remember so that I could tell others. He answered my prayer, and I have regretted it many times. There can be much pain in memory."

Short Feather was quiet and deep in thought for a few minutes. He then said, "I must say some things so that we understand each other. Truth is often hard to come by. A man can remember something clearly and be totally wrong. Events happen, battles happen, lives happen, and the truth of them is not always known. History is spoken or written by men with imperfect memories, perceptions, prejudices, philosophies, ignorance, arrogance, and many other traits that can influence their explanation or description of an event. In other words, what we hear or read as history may or may not be true or related accurately. Does this make sense, White Tears?"

"Yes, it does," Lee said. "And I believe that you are saying that I should listen to what you and others say but then check it against accounts from others who witnessed or knew of the event. I believe it is important to evaluate the person reporting or writing about the event to determine their motives and prejudices. That is why I did research after reading Standing Elk's story."

"That was good," Short Feather said approvingly. "Standing Elk's memory was tainted by a hate that he refused to let go. His story was correct, but he failed to mention that the white men who killed his family had been victims of an Indian raid that killed many of their family. That raid was in retribution for a previous raid, and so it went. It was a vicious circle, and no one was able to stop because of hate. Catastrophe was right around the corner when greed, pride, ignorance, arrogance, and bigotry were thrown in. The result was the almost-total annihilation of an entire race of human beings."

Short Feather went on. "Not all human beings are good, and not all are bad. Most are a combination of both, but I have found that there are some—Indian and white—who are totally evil. When they gain power, you see hell on earth. Hitler and Stalin would be good examples. Fortunately, they are few, and always die. A totally good person can make a difference that lasts forever. In all my studies and searches, I have found only one such person, and that is Jesus Christ of the Bible. He was killed, but I believe that He is alive. One more thing, before we judge others, we must first look to ourselves."

Lee looked at his hands then back at Short Feather. "Again, please do not be offended, but you are obviously prejudiced against white people. Yes, there are many who are bad in many ways, but I have found that most are good. You should not judge us all the same."

"You speak the truth wisely, White Tears," said Short Feather. "I stopped hating white people many years ago. Now it is a matter of trust. It is hard to trust when one has been deceived so many times and it appears that nothing has changed. To make my point, Lyndon Johnson is in the White House."

Lee was quiet for a moment and then said, "We all face the same dilemma, but I believe the key is love. We should love others, but that does not require trust. Love is something we should all choose, but it must be tempered with discretion. We are told to love our enemies. We are not told to trust them."

Short Feather turned to Rudy. "I like this white boy you have brought me, Chero." Then back to Lee, he said, "You have obviously been reading your Bible. Jesus taught about love."

"Can you both stay for dinner?" asked Short Feather. "Do you like pizza? It's my favorite thing to eat."

"I would love to," said Lee, "but only if you honor me by letting me buy."

"Done," said Short Feather. "What about you, Chero?"

"My wife will have my dinner ready," said Rudy. "I'm sorry, but I must leave soon."

Juanita came from the bathroom and started to collect her things. "I'm finished, and I need to go now to catch the next bus."

"Can you stay for pizza?" Short Feather asked her.

"I love pizza, but I don't like to be out after dark," Juanita replied.

"I'll take you home," said Lee a little too quickly. "I have my car, and it would be my pleasure."

Short Feather and Rudy looked at each other and smiled.

"Do you not have someone waiting for you at home?" asked Juanita.

"No, I live alone," said Lee.

Juanita blushed. "I will have to call my brother and let him know I will be late."

"After you call your brother, call and order the pizza," Short Feather said. "The number is in my Rolodex, under Fredrico's Pizza. He's white, but makes great pizza and delivers. Get pepperoni, sausage, mushrooms, olives, and tomatoes. Since White Tears is buying, let's live it up." He laughed.

3

> "One can tell more about a man by looking
> into his eyes than listening to his words."
>
> —Short Feather

After Rudy left and the pizza was ordered, Juanita sat next to Lee on the couch. Short Feather asked Lee to get a certain book from the top of one of the bookcases. He opened it and took out an old photograph of a soldier. On the back was written, "Silas Soule, 1864."

"I need to tell you about the time I met Silas Soule," said Short Feather. Picking up a small drum and a padded drumstick, he began to gently beat a rhythm that gave his words beautiful colors. He told his story slowly, clearly, and powerfully, enunciating and savoring every word like he was showing them precious gems.

His eyes were closed as he spoke.

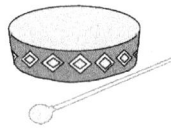

It was November 1864, and I was eight years old. My father and mother took my sister, Peppermint, and me to Fort Lyon on the Arkansas River. We were living in the village at Sand Creek about forty miles away.

I have not mentioned my sister. She was two years younger than me and was the sweetest child you could ever know. Father named her Peppermint because it was his favorite tea. My sister was small and beautiful, just the opposite of me. Her shiny black hair hung down to her waist. She had a smile and happy nature that made her a favorite in our village. I can see her now, in my mind, with the breeze blowing her hair and her deep-brown almost-black eyes looking out at a sunrise.

Fort Lyon in November was cold, windy, and dusty. We went there to trade some buffalo robes for supplies that Father needed for a hunt. The chief of the soldiers had told Black Kettle, our chief, to send his braves out to hunt and get meat for the winter, and that the village at Sand Creek would be under the protection of the US Army and the American flag that had been given to Black Kettle several years earlier.

There was an Arapaho village near the fort, and they appeared to be getting ready to move their village. Father said this was strange, as we went into the fort. We noticed that most of the soldiers were armed and seemed nervous. Then Father saw one soldier that did not have a weapon, not even a knife. He told Mother to take care of the trading.

Mother said scornfully, "You go and play, Laughing Wolf. Peppermint and I will do the work. She needs to learn the hard life of a Cheyenne woman."

Father walked directly toward the unarmed solder, smiled, and said in Cheyenne, "You do not have a weapon. There are Indians here that will think you are weak or stupid."

He then took his knife and sheath from his belt and handed it, handle first, to the soldier. The soldier obviously did not understand what Father had said but took a pouch of tobacco and gave it to him.

Father said, "No, no, it is a gift," and gave the tobacco back.

Now the soldier was even more confused and, looking around, summoned a young Cheyenne woman who lived at the fort. She spoke English well enough to help. Father was a little taken aback.

He knew the girl and did not approve of her profession but let her translate anyway. Her name was Snow Flower. The soldiers called her Daisy.

Father told Snow Flower what he had said and she told the soldier.

"I am Captain Soule," said the soldier through Snow Flower. "Thank you for the knife. I will keep it and treasure it. What is your name, and is this your son?"

Father smiled even more. He was not used to being treated like this by a white man, especially a soldier. "I am Laughing Wolf, and this is my son, Short Feather."

Captain Soule had a good face and kind gray eyes. He and Father talked and laughed for about a half hour before Mother and Peppermint came back. Mother did not look happy, but then she hardly ever did. She did have the supplies, and she and Peppermint stood a ways off, waiting.

I did not pay much attention to what Father and Captain Soule were saying. It was too confusing trying to listen to them and Snow Flower, so I sat down and drew pictures in the dirt.

Soon, Father tapped me on the back, and I stood up. Captain Soule looked directly into my eyes and said, "Short Feather, stay away from strong drink, the white man's firewater. Don't ever take even one drink. It will ruin your life and then kill you."

The kind and sincere look in his eyes pierced my spirit, and to this day, I have not taken a drink. It has been sad for me to see so many of my brothers destroyed by strong drink.

Another soldier came to Captain Soule and gave him a message. The captain became very serious and said to Father, "Please, you must take your family with you on the hunt. Return to Sand Creek, collect your belongings, and leave as quickly as you can. Major Wynkoop has been replaced by Major Anthony, and I do not trust him. He is not a friend of the Indians, as Major Wynkoop was. Also, Colonel Chivington and his troops are here. He is closing the fort, and the troops he brought are undisciplined. The colonel believes that all Indians are murderous savages. Now, please go quickly."

Father was agitated because Captain Soule had shown such great concern. He believed the captain and sensed danger. When we arrived at Sand Creek, Father told others what Captain Soule had said, but they just laughed at him and said that the soldier chiefs had promised to protect them.

Black Kettle would not leave. He had his American flag and his white flag that the soldier chiefs had told him to display in his village. Mother was also skeptical and thought that Father was being foolish. She always went on the hunts because of her talent but usually left Peppermint and me with our grandmother.

We packed up quickly and left early the next morning. By evening, we were many miles away. Two days later, we arrived at the hunters' camp. It was November 29, 1864—the day of the Sand Creek Massacre.

Many days passed before survivors began trickling into the camp. All were in terrible condition because they had walked over fifty miles in freezing weather with little warm clothing and hardly any food. Many were wounded. There was much wailing and sorrow, for everyone had lost a relative or friend. We were told that Grandmother had been killed, and Mother would have harmed herself had Father not lovingly restrained her.

The descriptions of the murders and atrocities were overwhelming. I want to forget everything I heard, but I cannot.

Black Kettle and his wife survived the attack, but she was badly wounded. He no longer had the respect of the tribe, and when his wife could travel, he left with a few faithful followers. I always believed in Black Kettle, that he was sincere in his efforts to achieve peace and lead his people. He never truly understood the evil that he was up against.

Silas Soule[1] saved Peppermint and me from almost-certain death. I only met him that one time, but he had a lasting effect on my life.

Mother gained a renewed respect for Father, and her attitude toward him changed until their deaths four years later. They became closer, and their love for each other grew.

Short Feather opened his eyes.

Juanita was quietly crying, and Lee had tears again. They were holding hands and didn't realize it. When they did, they quickly let go.

"I did not mean to upset you, Juanita," said Short Feather. "I am sorry."

"Oh no, please," she said. "I want to hear more of your life. Please do not stop."

"We will stop for now. The pizza should be here soon," said Short Feather. "White Tears, will you help Juanita get some Cokes and plates from the kitchen? I like to eat in my chair."

At that, Short Feather closed his eyes and went again to another place.

---

1   Silas Soule is the only real-life character that has a speaking part in this book. My account of him is fictional, but he was a very real and remarkable person. It is sad that he is little known or talked about today. There is a very good book written about him that I highly recommend. The title is *Silas Soule*, and the author is Tom Bensing. Check out the very good pictures included in the book. Be sure to look at the eyes of Silas Soule. The subtitle of the book is totally appropriate: *A Short, Eventful Life of Moral Courage*.

4

> "If life is hard and I need a rest, my mind
> can always take me to a better place."
>
> —Short Feather

When the pizza arrived, Short Feather opened his eyes and smiled broadly. With his first bite, he said, "I believe that pizza is one of the foods that we have gotten by divine intervention."

As they were eating, Lee asked, "Sir, what do you mean when you close your eyes and say you have gone to a better place? Is it meditation?"

"I suppose you could call it that," said Short Feather. "When I was very young, Father taught me how to control my body with my mind. He said his father taught him. It is simply a matter of thinking of something pleasant when you have to do something unpleasant, or you just want to calm your spirit, as I have just done."

Lee smiled. "I believe I know what you are talking about. I did the same thing when I was in the army, but can you give me some examples?"

"As I have said, I was larger, heavier, and stronger than others in my tribe," Short Feather said. "This sometimes made things difficult. If I was riding a pony, it would become tired faster than the others, so I usually had to run great distances. While running, I would, in my mind, go to a peaceful, quiet valley and lie under a tree by a beautiful river. This helped me to run."

Short Feather continued. "Once, another boy bet me that I could not carry a pony from one end of the village to the other. I picked up the pony and imagined that I was soaring like an eagle, high above the earth. Before I knew it, I was at the other end of the village."

"Yes, I used to do the same thing on long marches," said Lee.

Short Feather yawned. "This day has been special for me. It has been a long time since I have spoken of these things, and I have felt good about sharing them with you two. I am, however, becoming tired, and I think, White Tears, you need to get Juanita home. Will you please come again? I have much to tell you."

"I was hoping you would want me back," said Lee. "Would next Saturday be convenient? Can you get out? I'll take you to lunch."

"Anytime I get to go anywhere is a thrill at my age," Short Feather said. "Come about nine in the morning. We'll make a day of it."

"Hey, what about me, you two?" asked Juanita. "I like to get out too, and I want to hear more about your life, you inconsiderate old Indian."

"I'll pick you up about eight thirty," said Lee, laughing. "Now we need to clean up, and then I had better get you home."

Juanita and Lee cleaned up the kitchen while Short Feather made use of the indoor plumbing. When he came out, Lee shook his hand and said, "Thank you for letting me into your life."

Short Feather looked deeply into his eyes and smiled.

Juanita kissed Short Feather on the cheek and asked if he was okay.

"I will be fine, Juanita," Short Feather responded. "Just don't forget to come Thursday to clean."

"I love you," said Juanita as they left.

Juanita gave Lee directions, but they did not talk much. It was only about a fifteen-minute drive, and soon, Juanita said, "You must stop here, turn off your car, turn on the inside light, and roll down your window."

They were stopped in front of a three-story building, and Lee could see men on the roof looking down at them.

Soon, a young man came out to Lee's side. "Juanita, who is this gringo?"

"His name is Lee Grant, Roberto." she said. "He is a friend of Short Feather, the old Indian I clean for. It was getting dark, and he was kind enough to bring me home."

Roberto walked to the front of the car, wrote down the license number, and went back to Lee. Lee could not help but notice the revolver tucked into Roberto's belt.

"This is a nice car, a '57 Chevy," said Roberto, smiling. "My cousin and I have a shop. We could turn it into a great lowrider."

"I'll think about it," said Lee. "It is only nine years old."

"Will you be coming back here?" asked Roberto.

"I am going to take Short Feather and Juanita to lunch on Saturday. I'll be here at about eight-thirty."

"Always drive this way," Roberto said. "If the guard on the roof waves you on, go ahead. Otherwise, stop." He waved them on.

Lee asked Juanita as they drove, "What was that all about?"

"There are three rival gangs in Chino," Juanita answered. "Each has its own turf, and the guards are there to keep the others out. One would think things would be better in 1966. We are going to move out as soon as we can. Jose is looking at a house north of Pomona, but we would need to sell this one first."

They pulled up to a well-kept house about two blocks away from the guard station.

Lee got out and looked up at one of the guards who were watching him. Lee waved, and the guard turned and walked away. He was carrying a rifle.

As Lee was opening Juanita's door, a short husky man came out of the house. Standing at the front door was a woman holding a baby. The man, not smiling, looked at Lee first and then questioningly at Juanita.

"Jose, this is Lee Grant," Juanita said. "He was kind enough to bring me home. Lee, this is my brother, Jose Trujio."

"Lee Grant?" asked Jose. "Are you the Lee Grant who works at the testboard for the phone company?"

"Yes, I am," said Lee, somewhat confused.

"I'm Joe, an installer-repairman. We have worked together many times but have never met in person. It is good to meet you. Can you come in for a few minutes? I want you to meet my wife and baby."

"Just for a few minutes," said Lee, as they walked toward the house.

Juanita followed, wondering if they remembered she was there.

"Maria, this is Lee, the man I have told you about so many times," said Jose. "He makes my job easier by being really good at his. And, Lee, this is my wife, Maria, and our little girl, Anna."

"I am happy to meet all of you," said Lee. "And my foreman says that Joe is the best worker he has ever seen."

"Okay, you men," said Maria. "Enough bragging about each other. Lee, how did you meet Juanita?"

"Ah, someone knows I am here," said Juanita as she put away her things.

Lee told about Rudy, their visit, and that he was taking Short Feather out on Saturday for lunch and Juanita was coming too.

Jose chuckled. "You two just met, and already you have a date."

"It is not what you are thinking, Jose," said Juanita. "Lee offered to get Short Feather out of his apartment, and I said I was coming too. Short Feather is telling Lee about his life, and I don't want to miss any of it. He hardly ever talks about himself, but for some reason, he wants to tell Lee. I learned more about him today than I have in the past three years."

Lee got up to go. "I'll see you Saturday morning, Juanita. It has been great meeting all of you."

He waved as he drove past the guards. This time, they waved back.

5

"A beautiful song can lift our spirits to great
heights and fill us with wonder."

—Short Feather

On Saturday morning, Lee stopped at the guard building because they did not wave him on. A different man came out and walked around Lee's car, looking at it carefully.

He grinned and said with a deep Spanish accent, "My cousin Roberto said you would be coming this morning. We could do great things with this car. It would look magnifico with a candy apple-red paint job. Jose knows where the shop is. Come see us."

"I'll think about it," said Lee hesitantly.

Juanita was ready to go, and on the way to Short Feather's, Lee told her about Rudy's wife, Sara, and about Standing Elk's story.

"Thank you, Lee, for taking me along today," Juanita said. "I really do love that old Indian. I have always known that he had a difficult life, and I think it is good for him to talk about it. I will pay for my own lunch, of course."

"If you insist on that, I am going to take you back home," said Lee, laughing. "This day is on me, and I think it will be a good day."

Short Feather was dressed and ready to go. He wore tan pants with a big silver belt buckle. His shirt was a red-and-black cowboy shirt with a string tie. His shoes were penny loafers. Definitely an eclectic outfit, but he looked great, and still had the feather in his hair.

"That is a beautiful belt buckle," said Lee.

Short Feather took it off and handed it to Lee. "It is the End of the Trail and was given to me by the man who made it, a great-grandson of Chief Joseph. Read the inscription on the back."

Hear me, my chiefs! I am tired.
My heart is sick and sad.
From where the sun now stands,
I will fight no more forever.

Chief Joseph of the Nez Perce (1877)

Lee handed the buckle to Juanita.

Short Feather spoke. "Most people think that the End of the Trail was a painting, and indeed, there have been many paintings done of it. Actually, it was a sculpture done by a man named James Earle Fraser. He finished this version around 1916." He put the buckle back on.

"Okay, so where are we going?" asked Short Feather.

"I thought we could go to Puddingstone Lake near the fairgrounds," said Lee. "It has a nice park area, and it is a beautiful day to be outside. I know of a really good Swedish restaurant for lunch. I think you will like it."

Short Feather picked up a beaded leather bag that contained his drum.

At the lake, Lee took a folding lawn chair and a blanket out of his trunk and found a place in the park under a large tree. There was a nice breeze, and they could see the lake with a few boats and people swimming near the dam.

Short Feather sat in the folding chair and closed his eyes, breathing in the warm spring air. Lee and Juanita sat on the blanket.

"It is indeed a beautiful day," said Short Feather, "and it is nice to be out. I have felt good since we last talked, White Tears, and I am happy that you and Juanita are interested in my stories. After so many years, I never thought I would want to speak of my life to anyone because of the pain, but telling you two has freed my spirit. I do not understand it, but I gladly accept it."

"Please, can you tell us what happened after Sand Creek?" asked Juanita.

Short Feather took his drum, began to beat a gentle rhythm, and closed his eyes.

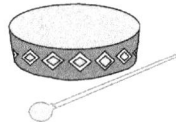

The next four years were difficult, but I look back on them as some of the best years of my life. Father and Mother decided to live apart from our tribe. Too many of the younger braves wanted to go to war against the white man, and my parents feared that the village would be attacked again.

We traveled into the mountains and found peaceful valleys, and although it was a hard life, we were never hungry because of the skill of my father and resourcefulness of my mother.

As a family, we were very close. Mother became a different person, smiling often and showing real affection for Father. Peppermint and I learned much from our parents. I learned many hunting skills, and my sister became every bit as good with a knife as Mother. It was amazing to see a little girl skin and dress out a deer quickly and cleanly with little effort or waste.

Mother would sing songs to us, and we discovered that Peppermint had a beautiful singing voice. They would make up songs together, and when they sang them for Father and me, our world would become quiet and peaceful. Peppermint's voice could lift our spirits to great heights and fill us with wonder. One of her songs has always been very special to me. I will tell you the words in English and then sing it in Cheyenne.

> The sun rises and the dark runs away,
> I rejoice and welcome a new day.
>
> The earth is warm
> The sky is clear
> I have no worry
> My family is near.
>
> A stream of clear water flows from the hill
> It quenches my thirst, and the sound keeps me still.
>
> The earth is warm
> The sky is clear
> I have no worry
> My family is near.
>
> This is my home in this valley of love
> I will always remember this gift from above.
>
> The earth is warm
> The sky is clear
> I have no worry
> My family is near.

A Negro couple with a sleeping baby stopped nearby. They were listening to Short Feather. Lee invited them to sit on the blanket, there was plenty of room.

Short Feather opened his eyes and smiled at them. Closing his eyes again, he continued speaking and softly beating the drum.

In the summer months, Peppermint and I would take our beds outside. We would lie on our backs, look up at the stars, and marvel at the amazing creation of the Great Spirit. When the moon was full, we talked about the fact that we could see it and it could see us, but what else did it see? We spent hours speculating on what the moon could see, and our imaginations filled our thoughts with wonders and beautiful places. We were young and had no idea. The truth was so much more, but also terrifying.

The winters were special for us. We spent many nights listening to stories that Mother had learned as a child. Sometimes she would just play her drum and sing softly until we fell asleep. I am grateful that the Great Spirit has given me the ability to close my eyes and hear that drum.

We spent three winters and two summers away from our tribe, but then my parents decided it was time to return. Near the end of the summer of 1867, we found Black Kettle and our Cheyenne people camped at the Arkansas River near Fort Larned. There was also a tribe of Arapaho. Living conditions were poor, but it was good to be with our friends again. Peppermint was especially happy to be with her friends after so long.

Many Cheyenne were still fighting the Long Knives in the north, and Black Kettle worked tirelessly to maintain peace where we were. It was an uphill battle because white people only heard bad things about Indians and we Indians could only remember Sand Creek. The Great Father in Washington and his council were breaking the treaties again. It was a hard winter, and food became scarce.

That summer, we moved on with Black Kettle, and in the autumn, he established a village on the Washita River. Many Cheyenne, tired of fighting, came from the north to join us. The nearest Long Knife fort was Fort Cobb, about one hundred miles away. There was an Arapaho village south of us as well as a Kiowa village and another Cheyenne village.

In the early morning of November 27, 1868, we were sleeping soundly in our lodge. It had snowed again, and was very cold. Peppermint spent the night with the family of one of her close friends.

At dawn, we were awakened by gunfire, and bullets were passing through our lodge.

Short Feather paused, the drumming stopped, and he bowed his head. His hands were shaking.

"Mother sat up, and I saw her head explode."

Juanita gasped.

Short Feather continued without the drum.

Father grabbed me and threw me outside, and we started running toward the river. There were gunshots coming from behind us, and I heard my father groan as he knocked me down, landing on top of me.

He said his last words—"Short Feather, pretend to be dead"—and he died.

Short Feather paused with tears on his face. He opened his eyes and looked up at the sky, then closed them again. He resumed his story, and the drumbeat started again.

My body and the snow were covered with Father's blood. I kept my eyes open, with a vacant stare, and watched as the soldiers killed every man and boy that they could find. When the soldiers were not looking my way, I crawled to some brush and then to the riverbank, where I hid and watched.

Many of the women and some children were collected by the soldiers. They loaded them into wagons, and I saw that one of them was Peppermint. She was only ten years old. That was the last time I saw her until almost twenty years later. She was only ten…years…old.

At the age of twelve, I was now totally alone. Everything in our village was burning, and I could hear our ponies being killed. Their cries sounded almost human, and I could take no more. It was quite cold, but I got into the river and let it carry me downstream. Soon, I saw a large number of braves coming from the other villages, but I did not hear much shooting. This did not make sense since our braves now far outnumbered the soldiers. Years later, I was told that the soldiers used the wagons full of women and children as shields.

I do not remember how I got there, but I found myself at the Arapaho village lying on a blanket, with an older woman removing a bullet from the back of my left leg about three inches above the knee. She was very gentle, and I think I was too cold to feel any pain. I called her Grandmother.

6

"Do not assume that you know a
man. He may surprise you."

—Short Feather

Short Feather was interrupted by three loud motorcycles coming into the parking lot. The men got off their bikes and stretched. They were all wearing black leather jackets that had a snake on the back with the word *Cobras*.

One of them was looking at Short Feather and his group. He started walking toward them. He was thinner than the other two and had mousy long brown hair and a Fu Manchu mustache hanging down below his chin.

"Snake, what the hell are you doing?" yelled the largest of the three. He had *Hugo* on the front of his jacket. "We don't have time for that. Just go to the head, and let's go."

Snake ignored Hugo and walked up to Short Feather. "Well, I'll be damned. Look what we have here: some niggers, a pretty wetback, a Twinkie, and a stink'n'-old Indian."

Both Lee and the black man started to get up, but Short Feather motioned for them to stay put.

Snake had a switchblade in his hand. "I ain't ever scalped me a Indian. How 'bout I just take that hair that you got that feather tied to?" The switchblade snapped open, and he approached Short Feather.

Hugo saw what was going on, shook his head disgustedly, got on his bike, and left with the other biker behind him.

Instantly, Snake was standing rigidly upright. Incredibly, the lower part of his mustache floated to the ground. Short Feather was holding the handle of his cane that had become a short very sharp sword. The point was up against Snake's throat.

"Now, Snake, I think you should stand very still," said Short Feather. "I am an old man, but all I have to do is raise my hand about eight inches, and I can carve my initials on the inside of your skull an instant before you die."

Snake turned white.

"Please drop the knife."

Snake hesitated, and Short Feather spoke further. "Snake, in my very long life, many soldiers, other white men, and more than a few Indians have tried to take my scalp. I learned quickly to ask only once for them to drop their weapons. Remarkably, most complied. Those that did not regretted their decision. I have had to defend my hair many times but have never had a single one taken from my head. That precedent will not end today."

Snake dropped the knife, and Lee picked it up.

"I want you to sit on the ground so that we can talk," said Short Feather, as he removed the blade from Snake's throat but kept it just inches away from his face. "I must really be getting old. I meant to take off the whole mustache but only got the part below your chin."

Short Feather was looking directly into Snake's eyes. "I think you need to apologize to my friends. You called them bad names and used profanity. Did you know that profanity is the language of the weak? You may apologize now."

Snake turned to Lee, Juanita, and the black couple. "I'm sorry, I was just foolin' around."

"Snake, you need to understand something: I just saved your life," Short Feather said. "White Tears—you called him a Twinkie, you're going to have to explain that one to me. Anyway, White Tears is just back from Vietnam. He was Special Forces, and they are taught to kill a man instantly with their bare hands. My point is that when you 'fool around' with someone, you need to know who you are 'fooling around' with. Life is very dangerous. Do you understand?"

"Yes, sir," said Snake.

"I like you, Snake," Short Feather went on. "I think I will call you Farting Horse, because that is what your motorcycle sounds like."

Juanita started to laugh but just cleared her throat.

"Would you believe that I used to ride a motorcycle, and can you guess what kind it was?" asked Short Feather.

"An...Indian?" said Snake.

"Good guess," said Short Feather. "Why did you call White Tears a Twinkie?"

Snake looked nervously at Lee and said hesitantly, "White on the outside, whiter on the inside, and soft, like a marshmallow."

Lee laughed and waved it off.

"You are fortunate, Farting Horse, that White Tears has a sense of humor," said Short Feather. "Now it is time for you to leave. Be careful, and remember, a rattlesnake missing its rattle is still a deadly rattlesnake. It is not something to play with. White Tears will give you back your knife."

As Snake rode away, Short Feather waved. Snake, sheepishly, waved back.

"I apologize for my behavior," said Short Feather as he put his cane back together. "I have not had so much fun for a very long time." He looked at the black couple. "We need to introduce ourselves. I am Short Feather. This Twinkie—I need to remember that—is White Tears, and this lovely young woman is Juanita."

"My name is Jacob Bronson, and this is my wife, Allison," said the black man.

Everyone shook hands.

"My husband is Dr. Jacob Bronson," said Allison. "I don't know why he does not tell people that."

Short Feather looked shocked for a moment but quickly regained his composure. No one seemed to notice.

"And the baby?" asked Short Feather.

"Her name is Clara Lee," said Allison.

"Clara Lee," said Juanita. "What a beautiful name."

Short Feather said that he was tired after telling his story about Washita, and his confrontation with Snake had not helped. "I think I would like to just sit for a while and enjoy this warm breeze." Then he closed his eyes and went away.

Lee, Juanita, Jacob, and Allison got up to walk around the park with Clara Lee still asleep in the stroller. The motorcycles did wake her, but she went right back to sleep.

"My real name is Lee Grant," said Lee.

"Interesting combination," said Jacob. "Did your parents have a reason for naming you that? And why does Short Feather call you White Tears?"

Lee smiled. "I don't think my parents, even now, realize the irony of my name, and Short Feather gives everyone he likes a new Indian name. He is probably thinking about your new names as we speak."

"What about Juanita?" asked Allison. "That does not sound like an Indian name."

Lee got a blistering look from Juanita. "She may tell you her Indian name, but I doubt it. Let's just say it is a bone of contention between her and Short Feather."

After circling the park, the group found Short Feather watching three small children playing with bubble makers. A small dog was trying to catch and eat them—the bubbles, not the children.

Short Feather looked at Jacob and asked, "Jacob, Allison said you are a doctor. Are you a medical doctor?"

"Yes, I am," Jacob answered. "As is my father and his father and his father, all the way back to my great-great-grandfather, who was a slave as a boy. He escaped the South through the Underground Railroad and ended up in an orphanage in Connecticut. All of the children there were encouraged to pursue higher education, and he became an MD. It seems to run in the family, and I have been very fortunate. My sister is an orthopedic surgeon."

Short Feather smiled in a knowing way, looking at Jacob as if he could see into his soul.

Jacob was confused and a little shaken by this. He said to Short Feather, "I wish we could stay longer and hear more of your story, but I am afraid we must be going. I need to check on patients at the hospital."

Short Feather said, "Before you leave, I must give you your names." He looked at Allison. "I will call you Warm Breeze, and your husband Healing Breeze, and the baby"—he paused—"Breeze."

After exchanging addresses and phone numbers, the Bronsons left.

Seated back on the blanket, Lee asked Short Feather, "Sir, you told Snake I was with the Special Forces in Vietnam. How did you know that?"

Short Feather sat up straight and looked deeply into Lee's eyes. "I did not know. I just thought it would impress him, so I made it up, I thought. You will need to tell me about that."

"I will, when I am able," said Lee quietly. "But we want to know what happened after Washita. You were interrupted by Snake."

"Where was I?" asked Short Feather.

"You said you were at the Arapaho village and an older woman was removing a bullet from your leg," said Juanita.

Short Feather took his drum, closed his eyes, and began again beating the drum gently.

We called all the older women of our tribe Grandmother. I called this woman my Arapaho grandmother but usually just

Grandmother. I told her what had happened while she worked on my leg. I did not know I had been shot until she showed me the bullet. She said it was not deep and had probably passed through my father's body before hitting me.

Grandmother was kind and had a beautiful smile. She told her son and his wife that I would be staying with them until my leg healed and then I would go and look for my sister. I had not thought that far, but she knew my heart.

With two small children, the family did not have much but shared what they had with me. Soon, I was able to get out and hunt. Using all the skills my father had taught me, we began to have more to eat and even some to share with other families. The tribe accepted me as one of their own, and I still hold all of them in a special place in my heart.

In the early spring, I left my Arapaho family. Grandmother cried, and so did I. I never saw her again. With only a blanket, a knife, a bow with a few arrows, and much determination, I walked north for many days. Later I figured out that I had walked over 150 miles.

I was tired one afternoon after walking since early morning. I heard a woman crying, sometimes screaming. The sound came from the other side of a small hill, so I walked in that direction. Soon I saw a large tree, and beneath it was a white woman standing in a hole about three feet deep. Her long dress was covered with dirt, and she was crying, shaking her clenched fists at the sky. She looked exhausted and, her hands were bleeding. Nearby was the body of a man. A blanket covered his face and the upper part of his body. There was a large dog lying next to the body.

The dog saw me and started to growl. Hearing the dog, the woman painfully crawled out of the hole and grabbed a double-barrel shotgun that was leaning up against the tree. I stayed where I was and decided not to move since the gun was aimed at my chest. Then the dog stopped growling, walked up to me, and started to lick my hand. He was wagging his tail. The woman said something

I did not understand. She had an amazed look on her face and then collapsed to the ground. She had fainted.

There was a wagon and horse nearby. I placed the woman on my blanket in the shade of the tree and found a jug of water and a piece of cloth in the wagon. After pouring some water on the cloth, I placed it on her forehead. The dog came and stayed by her side.

There was a shovel in the bottom of the grave, so I finished what the woman had started. When the ground level was at my shoulders, I stopped digging and climbed out. The woman and dog were both sitting up and staring at me. I went to the dead man and pulled his body to the grave. The woman got up and took some things from his pockets and a ring from his finger. She then took off his boots and motioned for me to place him in the grave, which I did. Taking a handful of dirt, the woman said something else and dropped the dirt onto the blanket covering the body. Weeping quietly, the woman collapsed again to the ground, but she had not fainted.

It did not take long for me to fill the grave. When I finished, I knelt down and sang a Cheyenne death song. The dog came and sat next to me.

> The Grandfathers told us that only the earth lasts forever.
> Now they are gone,
> The earth remains,
> They spoke the truth.

The woman did not understand Cheyenne, and I did not understand the white man's tongue. But I clearly understood, by the look on her face, what she said next: "Thank you."

Then she pointed at herself and said, "Maggie."

7

"It is not always necessary to hobble a horse…or a man."

—Short Feather

Short Feather opened his eyes to find a little girl about ten years old standing nearby and looking at his drum.

"Would you like to play my drum?" he asked.

She shyly nodded. "Yes."

The girl tapped the drum softly and gently, just as Short Feather had, and tears began falling from Short Feather's eyes.

Soon the mother came over. She waited and watched for a few minutes and then said, "Susan, it's time for lunch."

"Thank you, Susan," said Short Feather. "You have lifted my spirit by bringing to my memory a little girl I knew many years ago."

Susan said a quiet "Thank you," and went with her mother.

Short Feather put his drum back into the leather bag and said, "My stomach, the sun, and Susan's mother have told me it is time for lunch."

Lee and Juanita gathered up the blanket and chair. Walking to the car, Short Feather was stopped by Susan, who gave him a little yellow flower. She then ran back to her family.

Lee, Juanita, and Short Feather had a wonderful lunch. Afterward, they headed back to Short Feather's apartment.

Short Feather settled into his chair. Juanita and Lee sat on the couch.

"This has been a wonderful day," said Short Feather. "As I said before, telling you two my story has freed my spirit. Yes, there is much pain in memory, but I have also been led to remember many good times and people that I love to this day. There is joy in remembering."

Juanita said with a concerned look, "I know you must be tired, and we should probably go."

"Please stay a while," said Short Feather. "There is more that I wish to tell you, and I do not feel tired at all."

"I would love to hear more," said Lee, "unless you need to get home, Juanita."

"I'm a big girl, and I would love to spend this afternoon with two of my favorite men," said Juanita. She blushed a little when she realized what she had said. "You must tell us about Maggie."

Short Feather took his drum and began to beat softly.

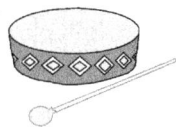

Maggie pointed at herself again and said, "My name is Maggie." She pointed at the dog and said, "Bruno, the dog's name is Bruno." Then she pointed at me with a questioning look on her face.

I told her my name. "Ka'e A'ke'Haso."

She looked bewildered and then said, "Ken, yes, your name is Ken," as she pointed her finger at my chest.

We put the shovel and gun in the wagon, and Maggie got up on the seat, looking sadly at the new grave.

Then she said, "Bruno, up," and Bruno jumped into the back. "Ken, get in." She pointed at the wagon, so I climbed into the back with Bruno.

"No, no," she said, and patted the seat next to her.

I moved to the seat, and she pointed at the reins and showed me her bloody, blistered hands. I had never driven a wagon before, but I knew enough from watching others to release the brake. The horse seemed to know what it was doing and headed toward the river.

Maggie started, right then, to teach me words of her language, like *horse*, *wagon*, *dog*, *tree*, and so on. She also made me tell her the Cheyenne word for each thing. We quickly began to understand each other.

After we had gone a short distance, we came to a clearing near the river. Six hobbled horses were grazing on the grass nearby, along with two cows and four oxen. There was a big Conestoga wagon and a wood platform built on stones about a foot off the ground. On the platform was a large tent of a fabric that I had seen before at the Long Knife camps. It was called canvas. I saw chickens in a fenced area and three or four more just wandering freely.

A cooking area was covered by another piece of canvas, and near it were two piles of wood. One pile was split for burning, and the other was unsplit. I remember this clearly because in front of the unsplit pile was an ax embedded in the ground. On one side of the blade was the body of a large rattlesnake, and on the other side was its head. I looked at Maggie, pointed at the snake, and then at the tree, where the man was buried. We could see it from the clearing.

She said, "Yes," and put her hand to her neck. I then pointed at the ax and then at her. She said, "No," and pointed at the tree. It was clear to me her husband had killed the rattlesnake before he died from being bitten in the neck.

We got down from the wagon, and Maggie went to the platform. There was a barrel on the platform, outside the tent, and Maggie filled a bucket with water from the barrel and went inside.

Bruno went to the snake and started to growl at the head. I said "Bruno" sharply, and he came to my side. Using the shovel, I picked up the snake's head, carried it toward the river, and buried it. I then used my knife to skin the snake body, laying the skin over a wagon wheel to dry, and threw the meat out for the birds to eat. Rattlesnake meat is very tasty, but I decided it had been in the sun too long and was not safe for us to eat.

The horse was still attached to the wagon, and looking at me, so I tried to figure out how to release it. After making a mess of things, I turned around and saw that Maggie had been watching me. Wearing a clean dress, with her hands bandaged, she was smiling and shaking her head. The horse was now looking at both of us and getting restless. Maggie showed me how to take off the harness, and soon, the horse was free to join the others.

I pointed at the horse and asked, "Name is horse?"

Maggie smiled again. "Her name is Blossom."

I pointed at Blossom's front legs and pretended to be hobbled.

Maggie said, "No, Blossom will not run away."

I understood "No," but not the rest. I could see Blossom would stay with the other horses.

The sun was now low in the sky, so I started a fire in the fire pit using some of the split wood. Maggie brought some dried meat and bread, and we ate. It was very good. I had been eating mostly rabbit, roots, and some berries for many days. When the night came and it was dark, Maggie went to her tent, and I spread my blanket near the fire. Bruno laid down on the platform in front of the entrance to the tent. I could hear Maggie crying.

Lying on my blanket, I looked up at the stars and thought about Mother and Father, and especially Peppermint. I wondered where she was and if she was now looking at the stars. I had not cried since I left my Arapaho family, but I cried now and decided to leave in the morning. I did not know that I would not leave Maggie for a very long time.

I awoke early in the morning, just as the sun was rising. Bruno had moved to sleep next to me. I did not know when, but was grateful for the warmth of his body. It was a beautiful morning, with birds singing and a light breeze moving white clouds across the sky.

After starting the fire again, I found a kettle and filled it with water from the barrel on the platform. I tried to be quiet but could hear Maggie moving around in the tent. There was a metal tripod with a hook by the fire pit, so I hung the kettle over the fire.

Then it hit me like a loud thunderclap. I remembered Father telling me that if there was one rattlesnake, there was usually another nearby. Taking the shovel, I started to prod around the woodpiles, and then I heard it. Bruno started to bark, and Maggie came out of the tent.

"Bruno, come," said Maggie.

He went and stood by her side, no longer barking but giving a low growl.

When Maggie heard the rattle, she put her hand to her mouth. I motioned for her to stay back. The snake was in the split pile of wood from which I had taken firewood. Looking around, I saw a long-handled pitchfork lying on the platform next to the tent. It worked well for moving the split wood without getting too close, and soon, I saw the snake when it struck at the pitchfork.

Moving quickly, I pinned the snake behind its head with the side of the pitchfork and kept it there by putting pressure on the handle with my foot. I motioned for Maggie to come and put her foot on the handle. Then I cut off the snake's head with my knife.

This snake was even larger than the one that killed Maggie's husband. I buried the head, skinned the body, and we had fried rattlesnake and eggs for breakfast. Maggie did not want to eat it, but after Bruno and I ate some, she did too. I think she liked it.

Juanita put her hand on Short Feather's arm and said, "Short Feather, stop. I have some questions."

Short Feather stopped the drum, opened his eyes, and looked at Juanita.

"What did Maggie look like? How old was she?" asked Juanita.

"Oh my," said Short Feather. "I can see her so clearly in my mind I did not think to tell you. She was about your height, Juanita, maybe a little taller and a little huskier. Her hair was red, and her skin was very white and dotted with freckles. Usually she was mild mannered and gentle, but if she ever got angry, you did not want to be the cause of that anger. I believe in 1869 she was twenty-three years old."

Lee asked, "What was her husband's name?"

"John, John Lawson," replied Short Feather. "Maggie's maiden name was Margaret O'Leary, and she had a scar over her left eye. She told me her father was a drunkard and hit her with a whiskey bottle when she was only twelve years old. Marriage was the only way she could get away from her father, so she married John when she was seventeen. He was twenty-nine. At first she did not love him, but grew to love him over time.

"John was a carpenter and lay minister. Maggie taught school. They moved from New Jersey to northeastern Kansas. John built houses in and around Topeka, and Maggie started a school. They did well, saved their money, and in 1866 set out for southern Kansas to start a new life raising chickens and eventually cattle. They never had any children."

"You were twelve years old when you met Maggie?" asked Juanita.

"Actually, I believe I was thirteen," said Short Feather. "My mother told me I was born in the Moon of the New Grass and the moon was full on the day I was born. I have since calculated that my birthday would be in the month of April 1856. In that month, the moon was full from the twenty-first to the twenty-eighth, so I picked April 26 as my birthday."

Lee was looking at Short Feather's drum. "Short Feather, is that a snakeskin wrapped around the body of your drum?"

"Yes, it is," said Short Feather, holding up the drum. "It is the skin of the snake that killed John Lawson. I made this drum and one other. It had the skin of the second rattler. I have had to replace the drumhead a few times, but the body of the drum is about ninety-seven years old."

"What happened to the other drum?" asked Juanita.

"I gave it to a little girl, but I must not get ahead of my story."

8

"One simple act of kindness can save a family, or build one."

—Maggie

Short Feather took his drum and closed his eyes.
"Wait, why do you close your eyes?" asked Juanita.
Short Feather looked puzzled for a moment, smiled, and said, "Do not mess with me, squirt."

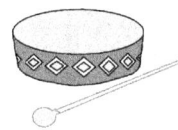

I decided to stay for a while and help Maggie with the farm. She was strong and always seemed to know what she was doing, but I could tell she felt overwhelmed. My desire was to find my sister, but I could not leave Maggie there alone.

Over the next several days, Maggie and I kept busy just taking care of the animals and learning to talk to each other. I found it amazing that she was able to learn Cheyenne faster than I learned English. We were creative, and it became like a game.

I finished splitting the wood and stacked it in a way that would make it difficult for a snake to hide. We now had plenty of firewood. Maggie always gave the stack a wide berth and would bang on it with the shovel before taking any wood. She taught me much about caring for the animals. Bruno and I were becoming great friends.

One clear morning, as the sun was coming up, I started the fire and began to heat water. Bruno started growling and was looking at the tree where John Lawson was buried. Sitting on his haunches and looking at us was a man. He looked like an Indian. The distance was about two hundred yards, and I could not see him well. Then I saw a woman carrying a child and leading an Indian pony that was pulling a small loaded wagon. The man put up his hand, and she stopped.

I turned to call Maggie, but she was already standing behind me, holding the shotgun. The man stood up. He was a big man, but seemed to sway a little, and I realized he was missing most of his left arm. The woman set the child in the wagon and took out a rifle. Seeing this, Maggie put the shotgun back in the tent, and the woman put the rifle away.

Maggie motioned for them to come. The man seemed to stumble and appeared to be very weak, so I ran to help him. As I got closer, I realized that he was a Dog Soldier and he had a pistol in his belt. The woman looked familiar to me. When I got to the man, he refused my help and walked toward the clearing resolutely, but with great difficulty.

Juanita interrupted Short Feather again. "Short Feather, you say the man was a Dog Soldier. I do not know what that means."

"Dog Soldiers were the military of the Cheyenne tribes," said Short Feather. "They were brave, strong, and well trained in battle and the art of killing. Respected and looked up to by all, they were also proud and often haughty. To say they were intimidating would be an understatement."

"Were you ever a Dog Soldier?" asked Lee.

"Yes, White Tears, and I still am, although my position now is honorary," answered Short Feather.

Short Feather continued his story.

The woman spoke to me in Cheyenne. "My brother is proud and even more stubborn. If he does not accept help, I am afraid he will not last this day. Please, boy, do you have any food? We have had little to eat in the last three days. Who is the white woman?"

As she spoke, I realized who she was. It had been over four years, but I recognized her voice more than the way she looked. Snow Flower was the young woman who translated for my father and Captain Soule at Fort Lyon. The child with her looked about three years old, and with the light curly brown hair and skin lighter than her mother's, I could tell that the father was obviously a white man.

I explained to Snow Flower about Maggie as we walked slowly behind her brother.

When we got to the farm (that is what Maggie called it), Maggie started to go to help the man, but Snow Flower said in English, "No, he would not like that. Just show him where to sit, please. His name is Thunderstorm, and he is my older brother. We were attacked by three white soldiers three days ago. They killed our father, and my brother killed two of them. The last one ran away after cutting off my brother's arm with a sword. I don't know how my brother has survived. He lost a lot of blood."

Maggie went to get a cup of water, but Thunderstorm would not take it from her.

"She is just trying to help," said Snow Flower angrily in Cheyenne as she took the cup from Maggie and gave it to her brother.

With a flustered then determined look, Maggie went into her tent and came out with a bag of coffee beans and a grinder. She sat near Thunderstorm, ground some beans, and made coffee. The smell of the coffee was wonderful, and definitely got Thunderstorm's attention. Maggie poured a cup and held it out for him. This time, he took it from her, but with a mere grunt. The coffee seemed to revive him a little.

Maggie gave some coffee to Snow Flower, who took it gratefully and said, "Thank you. You are very kind."

The child had not moved from the wagon. "My daughter's name is Sunrise. She is afraid of white people," said Snow Flower, as she picked the child up and placed her by Thunderstorm.

Maggie looked at me and motioned toward the chickens. I collected some eggs, and we cooked them up with some dried meat. Maggie even made some biscuits. There was enough for all of us, and as soon as we had finished eating, Sunrise and Thunderstorm were fast asleep. Snow Flower looked exhausted but did not want to sleep.

"We walked all night," she said.

"Your brother's arm, do you think it is infected?" asked Maggie.

"No," replied Snow Flower. "I cleaned it well, and I see no sign of infection, but the skin is loose. It needs to be sewn together, and I hope it is not too late." Then she explained to me what they were talking about. I understood all except the words *infected* and *infection*.

Maggie thought for a moment and then said, "I have needles and some good thread. I believe we need to deal with it as soon as possible. Do you think your brother will let us do what needs to be done?"

"Yes, he understands these things and knows that his life is in danger."

They decided to let Thunderstorm sleep. Maggie took Snow Flower to her tent and made her lie down. Then Maggie and I began to get things ready for our guests. I could see that the small wagon contained a buffalo-skin tepee but it lacked poles. After collecting enough branches from the trees by the river, I erected the tepee. This took considerable time, and when I finished, I found that Maggie had put the canvas on the Conestoga wagon, made two nice beds in it, and boiled water in which she sterilized the needles and thread. She was sitting on the platform, reading a book and praying.

When I unloaded the tepee from the wagon, I saw two more rifles beside the one Snow Flower had taken out. There was also a pistol, ammunition for all the guns, and a number of knives. I left all these weapons where they were and covered them with a blanket.

When the sun was getting high in the sky, Snow Flower came out of the tent. Maggie took her a bowl of hot water for washing and gave her a clean dress. Snow Flower had been wearing the only clothes she had for some time. When she came from the tent again, she looked very much the way I remembered. Her black hair was parted down the middle with two long braids. She was a small woman, but strong and with a bearing of authority. She reminded me of my mother.

The two women had been talking quite a bit, but I could not hear what they were saying. Sunrise woke up and started to cry when she did not see her mother. Bruno went to her and scared her a little at first, but when he lay down next to her, she began to pet his head.

Maggie went into the tent and came out with a small rag doll and a small blanket. She went to Sunrise and offered them to her. At that moment, they became good friends for life.

Then Thunderstorm woke up.

Snow Flower spoke to him and explained what needed to be done.

He said, "Do it now," and took off his shirt. These were the first words he had spoken.

"Short Feather, please take Sunrise for a walk, and don't come back until I call you," said Snow Flower. "If you hear screams, please cover her ears."

Sunrise did not want to go at first, but when I started walking away and Bruno followed, she came and took my hand. She was especially happy when I put her on my shoulders. There was not a sound from the farm for about an hour, and then we heard a shrill whistle. I took this to be the signal to return, so I carried Sunrise back, with Bruno running in circles around us. Sunrise squealed with delight.

Back at the farm, we found Thunderstorm sitting up on the blanket and eating some bread and dried meat. His arm had a new bandage. Maggie and Snow Flower were smiling.

"It went better than I expected," said Snow Flower. "My brother has endured more than I ever thought a man could endure."

Maggie sat on the blanket and started to cry. Thunderstorm put his hand on hers and said thank-you in English.

Short Feather stopped drumming and opened his eyes. "This has been a wonderful day. I would like to go on, but I feel I am taking up too much of your time."

Juanita looked at Lee and then at Short Feather. "I really would love to hear more. It is only three o'clock. Can we please stay a while longer?"

"Please go on," said Lee.

Short Feather looked pleased. "I will, but you must tell me when it is time to stop."

"Before you go on," said Juanita, "do you have a picture of Maggie?"

Short Feather picked up his Bible and took a picture from the back cover. It was of two women holding hands—one white, one Indian—and both dressed in calico dresses.

"This is Maggie and Snow Flower. It was taken in Dodge City in 1874," said Short Feather.

"They are beautiful," whispered Juanita.

"They were two of the most beautiful women I have ever known, inside and out," said Short Feather quietly.

He then took his drum and closed his eyes.

9

"Have faith in others, believe in yourself."

—Thunderstorm

Maggie sacrificed one of the plumper chickens the day that Snow Flower, Sunrise, and Thunderstorm arrived. We had a wonderful dinner of chicken and dumplings. Thunderstorm began to open up and looked much better. He said that his friends called him Storm and we should now call him that. Snow Flower said we should just address her as Snow.

Maggie said that Snow and Sunrise would sleep in the tepee and Storm and I could have the beds in the Conestoga. Storm still had his pistol and two knives that I had not seen before. He also took one of the rifles and said that it was mine and that I should keep it with me at all times. This seemed a little strange since he did not give me any bullets.

The beds were very comfortable, and Storm was asleep almost instantly. Bruno jumped in with us, and soon, both he and Storm were snoring loudly. This made it hard for me to sleep, so I took my bed and rifle and slept in the kitchen under the canvas since it looked like it could rain. John Lawson had put a wood floor there, so I was quite comfortable.

I woke at sunrise, with Bruno licking my face. Storm was already up and, for some reason, was wandering around the farm looking at everything. I went to ask what he was looking for.

Storm looked at me and said, "I see you have your rifle. That is good."

"Why do I need to have my rifle with me when I do not even have one bullet?" I asked.

"There will be a time for that. Do you know why John and Maggie chose this site for the farm?" asked Storm.

"No, I do not. Is there something wrong?" The instant I asked the question, I began to see what Storm was seeing.

"We need to talk to Maggie, and then we are going to kill a buffalo," said Storm as he walked back to the fire pit.

After breakfast, Storm talked to Maggie, with Snow's help. He told her that her farm would be flooded two or three times a year and that everything could be washed away with very little warning. The farm was simply too close to the river and was on a floodplain. Maggie asked how he knew this, and he pointed out the sandy areas and the watermarks on the trees. He also told her that a storm, many days away, could cause the river to rise. Snow confirmed everything that Storm had said and told Maggie that she needed to move everything to a better location.

Maggie looked around and finally said with her hands on her hips, "We have only been here for about a year after looking at many locations. John loved this place. The river did rise a month ago, but the water never got this far. Oh, dear me!"

Storm then said to the women, "You two need to think and talk about this. Short Feather and I are going to kill a buffalo. We need fresh meat and a good buffalo robe and everything else the animal will provide."

Storm went and looked at the work wagon that I had driven before. "Maggie, can we use your wagon and a horse to pull it?"

"Yes, of course," said Maggie. She was still looking around at the farm, the river, and trees. She was confused and overwhelmed.

I went to get Blossom. She came with me willingly, and I harnessed her to the wagon.

Snow brought us some dried meat and bread. Storm went to his small wagon and brought back one bullet.

"This is all you will need, Short Feather," he said with a smile.

I could tell that his arm was hurting him but he did not want to show it.

"Uncle, I do not want to tell you this, but I have never fired a rifle. I have only used a bow to kill rabbits and birds. How am I to kill a buffalo with only one bullet and my first shot? Where is this buffalo that I am to shoot?" I thought these were reasonable questions.

"You are young. Have faith in me, and believe in yourself as much as I do." This Storm said, looking directly into my eyes.

We climbed up on the wagon and headed out with the morning sun on our backs. Storm asked me about my parents and how I had come to be with Maggie. I told him about Washita and how my parents and so many others had died. I told him about the women and children being loaded into wagons and taken away. I told him about Peppermint and that I was going to find her. I told him about digging the grave and how Maggie had taken me in. Then he asked me my father's name.

When I told him, he looked at me for a long time and said, "Laughing Wolf was a great man. I knew him when we were young. Did you know that he was asked to be a Dog Soldier?"

"No, I did not know that," I said.

"Your father said that he believed with Black Kettle that we could live in peace with the white man," said Storm. "I told him that the white man could not be trusted and we must kill them all before they killed us. It causes me great pain to know that I was right." He was quiet for a long time, as Blossom pulled us along.

Storm began to talk again. "The Long Knife Chief that led the attack at Washita was the one we call Yellow Hair. His white name is George Armstrong Custer. Do not forget that name. He killed your parents. It is said that he attacked your peaceful village by mistake and that he meant to fight the more belligerent Cheyenne village farther down the Washita. I do not believe it was a mistake. I believe he wanted the women and went for the easier target. If you ever find your sister…" He did not finish what he was saying.

Storm was quiet as the sun continued to rise in the sky. When the sun was almost directly above, he said to stop, and he climbed down from the wagon and told me to get down. He said he had seen signs of a small herd of buffalo in this area four days before. Then he took my rifle and taught me how to load it. Drawing pictures in the dirt, he talked about the sights, how to line them up, and where to aim on the buffalo, just behind the shoulder. He said I should take a deep breath, let it out, and gently squeeze the trigger.

I practiced shooting in my mind, firing many times, and never missed once even though I never actually fired a shot. Storm said my body and mind could not tell the difference between imagination and reality. He gave me the one bullet, and I loaded the rifle.

We walked ahead of Blossom, and soon I saw the tracks of buffalo. It looked like a small herd of about twenty. The tracks were fresh. Setting the brake on the wagon, we walked about two or three hundred yards until we came to a low ridge. Then we crawled forward. I could tell that Storm was having a hard time. Below us was the herd of buffalo. One animal was smaller and closer to us, farther up the rise than the others. Storm signaled for me to shoot that one.

I aimed as he had taught me and, as I had practiced, took a deep breath, gradually let it out, and gently squeezed the trigger. The rifle fired, pushing hard into my shoulder. The buffalo did not move for what seemed to be a very long time and then crumpled straight down to the ground.

We got up and walked to the animal. It was dead, for I had shot it exactly where Storm had told me. Storm said that one of the bigger ones would have been too heavy for the wagon, and that was why he had me shoot this smaller one.

Then Storm gave thanks to the Great Spirit and the spirit of the buffalo. Turning to me, he said, "Short Feather, you are now the arm that has been taken from me. If you let me, I will teach you how to survive in this world."

After gutting the animal and saving the heart, liver, and kidneys, we were able to get it into the wagon, which strained under the weight. Blossom did a good job pulling the wagon, but we could tell it was difficult for her. Storm and I decided to walk beside her. I felt exhilarated and happy with what I had done and learned. Storm seemed to be feeling better and walked taller and straighter. It was going to be a long walk to get back to Maggie, Snow, and Sunrise.

The sun was bright and the sky was clear except for a few white clouds. There was a cool breeze that made the walk pleasant. Two hours later, Storm suddenly stopped, motioned for me to stop, and then pointed at some trees and bushes. At first I saw nothing but then saw something move among the bushes. It appeared to be a small animal, walking on all fours, but it was wearing clothes.

Setting the brake on the wagon, we walked toward the trees. As we got closer, we could see it was a small Indian boy digging roots.

Storm said, "Boy, are you alone?"

The boy was clearly of the Cheyenne, and jumped when Storm spoke.

"Do not be afraid, we will not hurt you," I said with a smile. "Are you alone?"

"My mother and grandmother are that way." He pointed in the direction that we had been walking. He was thin and looked weak.

"How long since you have eaten, boy?" asked Storm.

The boy began shaking, and said, "I do not remember. We are all hungry and have no food. Mother sent me to find roots, but I don't know how." He began to cry.

I asked how old he was, and he said eight winters.

Storm put the boy on the seat of the wagon, gave him some dried meat and bread, and told him to show us where his mother was.

It was a short distance, and we found a gully just up from the river. There were eight women and three more children all huddled in some bushes. They looked like they were starving. I quickly sliced the buffalo liver, and all but two of the women gratefully began to eat. Raw liver is very nutritious, and even the children began eating. One woman said that this was the first real food they had had in four or five days.

Rain Catcher, the boy we found, was the only one of the group strong enough to find food, but he was very young and had not found much. His mother's name was Sage Woman, and she told us what had happened while Storm and I built up the fire to cook the heart and kidneys.

They came from the north to join Black Kettle and his people. Their men were tired of fighting, and it was becoming more difficult to find food and shelter. When they got to the Arkansas River, they were attacked by the Long Knives, and all the men were killed or taken captive. Everything they had was taken or burned by the soldiers. The women and children were left to starve.

Rain Catcher's grandmother and one other woman were so weak they could not eat the liver. We tried to feed them some bread soaked in water, but this did not help much.

The grandmother died. Her last words were, "Please save the children."

The four children were all very weak. One could hardly hold her head up. It was hard to see human beings in this condition. My hate for the Long Knives increased.

Storm decided that I would take the children to Maggie and Snow with Sage Woman and the other woman who was so weak. At this point, it was about a two-hour trip. He would stay with the others until I returned. The buffalo meat would stay since the remaining women knew what to do with it. Storm said I should not try to come back until morning. It was already late afternoon.

Short Feather stopped drumming and opened his eyes. "I believe we should stop here. I am growing tired."

"Tomorrow is Sunday," said Lee. "Would it be all right if Juanita and I came to spend the day with you? We want to hear more of your story."

"Oh, yes, could we, please?" begged Juanita. "You can't just leave us wondering what happened next."

Short Feather smiled. "It amazes me that two young people would want to spend so much time with an old man. Yes, of course you may come. But before I go on, I want to hear your story, White Tears. Are you ready to tell it? I sense that you need to."

"You are right again, sir," said Lee. "I am just not sure I am ready."

"I am always up with the sun," said Short Feather. "You two come whenever you want."

As Lee drove Juanita home, he did not realize she was looking at him in the same way a person would study a work of art.

10

"People say, 'War is never the answer.'
I ask, 'What is the question?'"

—Short Feather

Lee and Juanita agreed to go to Short Feather's early, and when Lee arrived at 8:00 a.m. to pick her up, Juanita was ready to go. They stopped on the way, and Lee bought a large box of fresh doughnuts. On entering the apartment, they found Short Feather sitting in his chair and a black man sitting on the couch. Both were holding Bibles.

"White Tears, Juanita, this is Charles Ridley," said Short Feather. "He lives in an apartment upstairs. I call him Charley."

Charley stood up, and everyone shook hands.

"Every Sunday morning, we do a Bible study and pray," Short Feather went on. "You may stay if you like, or go for a walk. We'll be about a half hour. If you go for a walk, you may leave the doughnuts. They smell really good."

"I would like to stay and listen, if it is okay," said Lee.

"I want to stay too, but I'll put the coffee on first," Juanita said, heading for the kitchen.

Charley was sixty-five years old, about five foot ten, with all-gray hair and a thick mustache. He was retired from the US Navy, spending most of his career as a captain's steward.

"I like your young friends, Short Feather," said Charley. "They brighten the room and bring good things to eat."

Juanita returned and sat next to Charley. Lee brought a chair from the dining area.

Charley cleared his throat. "Let us pray. Father, as we open Your Word, we ask You to bless this time that we spend together and with You. We also ask that You open our hearts and minds to the instruction and interpretation of Your Holy Spirit."

Short Feather opened his Bible to the book of Matthew, chapter 13, starting with verse 24. It was the parable of the wheat and the tares, and he read to verse 43. Then Short Feather and Charley discussed the passage at great length. Lee was amazed at their insight and clarity of thought.

When they finished, Juanita brought in the coffee and opened the doughnuts. Both Short Feather and Charley took doughnuts frosted with chocolate.

After the coffee and doughnuts, Charley excused himself. He was going to go to church and spend the day with his son's family.

Short Feather took another doughnut, finding the last with chocolate frosting. Lee made a mental note for next time.

Picking up Short Feather's Bible, Lee began leafing through it. There were many underlined passages and notes in the margins. "Sir, I have read that many Indians despise Christianity, the white man's religion, and yet you study the Bible. Are you a Christian?"

Short Feather became thoughtful and spoke slowly and carefully. "I suppose you could call me a Christian although it is difficult to pin down what it means and what it is. Many people who call themselves Christians do not know Jesus or even try to follow His teachings. I call myself a messianic believer. I believe that Jesus, of the Bible, is the Jewish Messiah, the Son of God who came to earth, became man, was killed, and yet lives even today.

"I have found that the Great Spirit of my ancestors and the God of the Bible are totally compatible and the same God. Jesus is my Lord. In everything I do, I strive to follow His teachings. I fail often and have much to learn, but He knows my heart and loves me because He chooses to. I believe because I am one of His sheep.

"Now I would like to hear your story of your time in the army. Are you ready, White Tears?"

Juanita had been listening carefully to everything but remained quiet, looking at Lee.

"I believe I am," said Lee. "I have told no one of this incident except in official army reports that are sealed."

I joined the army out of high school in 1960. After boot camp, I was asked if I would be interested in the Special Forces. It was an honor, and I accepted. The training was difficult and intense, but I was determined to excel and advance. By 1962, I was a staff sergeant and was sent to Vietnam as an adviser to a South Vietnamese unit. I cannot go into detail about people and places because much of what we did is still classified.

The unit I advised was an operational unit, and our mission was to determine the status of the Viet Cong in certain areas and the amount of support provided by the civilian population. This meant that we checked many villages for supplies and weapons that were intended for the enemy. If such were found, the village was simply destroyed. The people were interred and interrogated—the ones that survived, that is. I saw little compassion or mercy.

On one occasion, we spent a number of days with one village that I believed was loyal and friendly to the South Vietnamese government. No arms were found, and there was no evidence of VC support. The people were great, and I especially enjoyed the children. The commander of the unit I was with, however, determined that the village needed to be eliminated since it was in a strategic location. The people were to be relocated. I objected strenuously and prevailed. We left the village intact and returned to base.

Three days later, we received information of VC activity in the vicinity of that same village. On returning, we found it completely destroyed with the bodies of men, women, and children everywhere. The VC had killed and destroyed because we left the village intact, and therefore, the VC assumed that the villagers were friendly to us. I felt totally responsible and was no longer able to perform my duties properly. I returned home and left the army in 1964.

Short Feather looked at his hands. "It is sad that we never learn, nor are we able to change. War is sometimes necessary to achieve peace, but…"

Short Feather was unable to finish his sentence. "White Tears, I am sorry you had to go through that." He closed his eyes and went to another place.

Lee and Juanita sat quietly, holding hands.

11

"When others become nothing to
me, I am already nothing."

—Short Feather

Ten minutes later, Short Feather took his drum, closed his eyes, and continued his story.

When I returned to the farm, I found that Maggie and Snow had started to get ready to move. Maggie agreed the farm was in the wrong place. I told them what had happened.

Sage Woman told us that the older woman and the weak little girl were dead. Maggie and Snow tended to the survivors and prepared some food. It was a very difficult time. That night, I cried myself to sleep.

I awoke before sunrise with a grim determination to seek revenge, and prepared to leave taking ten rounds of ammunition for my rifle. Maggie brought me some food and her dead husband's hat. She kissed me on the forehead, placed the hat on my head, and said, "You and Storm must return quickly. We need you now more than ever."

The trip back to the gully seemed to take forever, but Blossom was well rested and set a good pace. I just let her take over and let my mind wander until I heard gunshots. We were close to the gully. I stopped Blossom and set the brake.

Crouching low, I ran to the gully and saw Storm with four of the six women huddled among some rocks. Two women were on the ground and not moving. Some Long Knife soldiers were at the mouth of the gully and moving toward Storm and the women. I only saw two. Then I saw Storm raise a white cloth tied to a stick. He stood and started walking toward the soldiers.

My eyes caught some movement on the other side of the gully, which was not wide. A third soldier was crawling to the edge. He was behind and above Storm but lower than me, and had a rifle just like mine pointed at Storm's back.

One of the women saw the third soldier and yelled, "Behind you!"

Storm jumped to his right just as the soldier fired. The bullet could not have missed by more than an inch. As Storm ran back to the rocks, the soldier was reloading. He had a clear shot into the rocks.

I aimed my rifle at the soldier, took a deep breath, and let it out slowly as I squeezed the trigger. The soldier's head disappeared in a cloud of red. It did not take long for me to reload as the other two fired their rifles in my direction. The shots were low, and I felt them impact the slope in front of me. Again I aimed carefully, following Storm's instructions, and shot the soldier on my right in the chest. The other began to run away. I shot him in the back.

At the age of thirteen, I killed three men in less than two minutes. I felt sadness for my sisters who had died. I felt nothing for the soldiers. To me, they were just deadly animals that needed to be put down.

Storm and the women ran to the two women on the ground. Storm checked them and began to sing a death song as the surviving four women cried. When I reached them, Storm just looked at me with a look of sorrow and desperation that I will never forget.

I noticed one of the women had Storm's revolver, which she handed to him. When he saw me watching, he said, "I told them to kill themselves if I died. There were four bullets left."

Lee interrupted Short Feather, who stopped drumming. "Sir, you said that you felt nothing for the soldiers. You felt nothing?"

"White Tears, to me they were nothing," Short Feather responded. "Nothing more than that rattlesnake I killed at Maggie's farm, a danger that needed to be destroyed. It was many years before I realized that most white soldiers viewed Indians the same way."

"Short Feather, I am so sad that you had to go through all of that," said Juanita. "Do you believe the women would have killed themselves?"

Short Feather looked at Lee and then Juanita. "Yes, I believe they would have. All of them had witnessed what happened to Indian women captured by soldiers. This has been the same throughout history. The women of the defeated always suffer the most."

Short Feather closed his eyes again and went away. Then without opening his eyes, he began again to beat the drum softly.

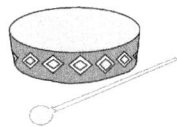

After collecting the weapons, ammunition, and anything else of use from the dead soldiers, we removed the saddles and harnesses from their horses and set them free. Storm did not want to keep the horses because they were too easily recognized as US Army property.

We put the bodies of the dead women into the wagon with the survivors and started for Maggie's farm, leaving the dead soldiers where they died.

When we arrived at the farm, Maggie and Snow were standing between the tepee and the Conestoga, looking at a hill on the other side of the river. Maggie was holding her shotgun, and Snow held a rifle. There was a man sitting on a horse looking down at the farm. He was wearing the shirt and hat of a Long Knife uniform but looked like an Indian.

"He is a Crow scout for the Long Knives," said Storm, as he spat on the ground.

Then the man turned and rode away, disappearing behind the hill.

We got down from the wagon, and little Sunrise came running toward me. I dropped to my knees, and she wrapped her arms around my neck, hugging me for a very long time. Bruno was by her side, licking my hand. That was one of the best moments of my life.

I spent the rest of the day building four high platforms on the hill by the tree where John Lawson was buried. We placed the dead little girl with her mother, who was one of the women killed by the soldiers.

The next morning, we disassembled the tent platform and kitchen floor and loaded the lumber on the wagon with the tent and teepee. The chickens were put into cages, and by midafternoon, we were ready to move. With the oxen pulling the Conestoga, Blossom with one other horse pulling the work wagon, and the pony pulling Storm and Snow's wagon, we headed west.

We made quite a sight with a white woman, a one-armed Indian man, five Indian women, and four Indian children. There was also one very young and angry Cheyenne boy.

12

"Wisdom begins with understanding."

—Snow Flower

We traveled toward Fort Dodge. Maggie knew a captain there and believed she could trade for supplies. When Storm was not instructing me in the art of fighting, Maggie and Snow were teaching us English, and we were helping Maggie with her Cheyenne. The women and children we had rescued were recovering from their ordeal, and pretty much stayed to themselves.

Our caravan was slow, and on our second day, we were approached by four soldiers. Three were Crow scouts, and one was white. One of the scouts looked like the one we had seen on the hill near Maggie's farm.

As they approached, Storm said to me, "Follow my lead," and when I looked at him, he began to transform into an imbecile before my eyes. I could not believe it. He undid his hair and let it fall around his face, which was contorted, and his head drooped to one side. He even drooled.

When the soldier and scouts reached us, they made all of us stand together away from the wagons. I did not like the way they were looking at Maggie, Snow, and the other women. Getting angry, I started to move toward them when Storm whispered, "Wait." He was shuffling, dragging his left leg and letting his arm dangle. I knew he had two knives hidden under his shirt.

The white soldier went to Maggie and said, "Lady, what're ya doing with these stinkin' savages?"

One of the Crow scouts grabbed Snow and held her arms behind her back. Little Sunrise began to cry as she clutched her doll close to her chest and stood by her mother.

"We are going to Fort Dodge," said Maggie. "These people are human beings, and you should treat them as such."

The soldier sneered. "Yer a rotten Injun lover and they're Cheyenne. As fer as I'm concerned, they're vermin in need of 'sterminatin', but we's thinkin' we'll have a little fun first."

Maggie had tied Bruno to the wagon, and he was snarling and pulling at the rope.

The white soldier pointed at me and said to the scouts, "One a ya Crow take care of the kid. I dun like da way 'e looks at me. And kill that dog."

The largest scout pulled his knife and walked toward me.

Storm started to giggle and dance on one leg, dragging the other. He yelled, "Fun, fun, fun!" and stumbled toward the white soldier. In an instant, one of Storm's knives was in the soldier's chest and his second knife was at the throat of the third scout, who started to reach for his pistol but stopped.

I dodged the thrust of the scout coming at me and tackled him. We both went to the ground. He ended up on top of me with his knife just inches away from my throat. He was strong, and I thought I was going to die when I heard a crack, and he fell off me, dropping his knife. Eight-year-old Rain Catcher had hit him in the head with a rock. I picked up the Crow's knife, and—he died.

The scout who had been holding Snow let go of her to help his partners. He was now on the ground, dead. Snow had plunged her knife into his back with all the strength she could muster. Little Sunrise had been holding the knife behind her doll.

Storm still had his knife at the last man's throat with the point just under his chin. He said in Crow, "You can put your hands over your head, and I might let you live. If you go for the pistol, you will die."

He started to pull the pistol, and died.

"Sir, please, I have a question," said Lee. "Storm taught you to always have your rifle with you, yet neither you nor Storm had a gun when the soldiers rode up. Why was that?"

"Thank you, White Tears," Short Feather said. "I did not mean to leave that part out. When we saw the soldiers coming, Storm said to leave our guns hidden. He did not want to get into a gun battle with the women and children so close."

Storm told Maggie and Snow to take the women and children and keep moving. We switched one of Maggie's horses for the Indian pony that had been pulling Storm's small wagon, and Storm told Rain Catcher to drive it. Storm also took a shovel from the Conestoga.

"Short Feather and I need to make this look like the soldiers were attacked by a band of renegade Indians," said Storm. "We will not be long, and will catch up as soon as we can."

When the wagons were out of sight, Storm scalped the four men. He took their boots and tied them to the army horses, putting the scalps in a saddlebag along with the bloody rock that Rain Catcher had used. Giving me the saddlebag, he said he would take the horses as far away as he could and release them. My job was to ride the pony around the site to make it look like a battlefield with many Indians. Then he said something I did not understand until later.

"Leave our wagon tracks, but be sure to wipe away any of our footprints." He also said, "Take the saddlebag and bury it where it will never be found."

Storm mounted the horse that Maggie had given him to use and led the army horses south. Finishing my job, I took the saddlebag and shovel and rode south, following Storm's tracks. It must have been two or three miles when I came to a creek that Storm had crossed. I rode up the creek for a ways and then headed northwest to find Maggie and the others. On the way, I buried the saddlebag.

When I found Maggie and the others, they had stopped for the night and were making dinner only a few miles from where our battle had taken place. Storm did not arrive until almost midnight. He said he had gone back to the site after releasing the horses.

"About twenty soldiers are there, and they have buried the dead," said Storm. "The leader is an officer and was studying our tracks. They will be here in the morning, probably before sunup. I think it would be best if Short Feather and I are gone."

Storm took Maggie and Snow aside and told Maggie what to say to the officer. We gathered up all the weapons and ammunition we had taken from the soldiers and used the small wagon to move them to some rocks and brush that were about a hundred yards from the wagons. The small wagon had to go back since our tracks showed the Conestoga and two other wagons. Covering our footprints and wagon tracks as we went, we walked to the rocks and used the brush to hide ourselves and the weapons.

It was a beautiful clear night, and the moon was almost full. Lying on my back and looking at the moon, I thought about Peppermint again. Where was she, what was she doing, what was happening to her? Thinking of my sister caused my heart to ache and filled me with anger and hate.

Just as Storm predicted, the Long Knives came riding up our trail as the sun peeked over the horizon. We now had eight rifles just like mine and about 150 rounds of ammunition. Taking positions about twenty feet apart, Storm and I each had four loaded rifles and a clear line of sight.

Storm put a blanket in the cleft of a rock to support his rifle since he had only one arm. Using some brush to hide it, he looked at me and said, "Short Feather, you are four for four with your rifle. Remember what I taught you and that missing is a waste of ammunition. Do not shoot unless I do. I hope we will not have to fight on this day."

As the soldiers approached, it looked like Maggie, Snow, and Sage Woman were making breakfast. Storm had said for the other women and children to stay in the Conestoga. The officer got off his horse and walked up to Maggie, and they began talking. Four other soldiers dismounted and started checking the wagons, making the women and children get out. The only weapon they found was Maggie's shotgun.

Maggie poured herself a cup of coffee and one for the officer. They talked for about ten minutes, with the officer pacing and sometimes pointing and waving his arms in a frustrated way. The four soldiers finished checking the wagons, and one talked to the officer as the others remounted their horses. Then the officer threw his cup on the ground, started to walk away, turned back to Maggie, and yelled something else, looking very angry. When he was finished, he got back on his horse and headed back down the trail with his troops following.

Storm gave a great sigh of relief and said, "For a white woman, that Maggie is remarkable."

Short Feather stopped drumming and opened his eyes.

"Short Feather, what did Maggie say to the officer?" asked Juanita impatiently.

"You are getting pushy, my little Buffalo Tail," said Short Feather, chuckling. "I'm getting to that. Snow told us all about it. But now I am going to excuse myself before I have another cup of coffee. So you will just have to wait."

When Short Feather came back, Juanita poured him another cup of coffee and kissed him on the forehead before sitting back down.

Short Feather looked into what was left of the doughnuts but did not take one.

The drumming resumed.

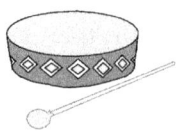

Once the soldiers were out of sight, Snow took a horse and set out to follow them to make sure they were not going to return. After about an hour, she returned and signaled us to come back to the wagons. Rain Catcher brought Storm's wagon to take back the weapons and ammunition. He was dressed to look like a little girl—and did make a cute little girl at that—but judging by his angry and embarrassed look, Storm and I decided not to say anything.

As we finally ate breakfast, Snow told us what Maggie and the officer had said. Little Sunrise came and sat on my lap, with Bruno next to us. The officer's name was Capt. Joseph Evens, and Maggie had met him before. The captain and Maggie's husband, John, had been friends.

"Maggie?"

"Captain Evens."

"Maggie, what is going on? Where is John?"

"John is dead. He was killed by a rattlesnake bite to his neck."

"Oh, dear God in heaven, I am so sorry. But what are you doing with these savages?"

"They were left to starve by your army. I am trying to help because they are human beings. They are people, not savages."

"Your wagon tracks went right past four of my men who were dead on the ground. Did you not see them?"

"Of course we did."

"But you just left them there?"

"What was I supposed to do? I had four sick and weak women and four little children that had been almost starved to death."

A soldier nearby said, looking at Sunrise, "One a dem little girls looks to be almost white."

A second soldier said, "Yeah, squaw's rape easy."

There was snickering among the men.

Evens said, turning to his men, and very angry, "You fools need to learn when to keep your mouths shut. This is one of those times."

"Captain, why are you here?" asked Maggie.

Turning back to Maggie, Evens said, "Those men were AWOL, deserters. We came looking for them. They bragged about what they were going to do to… And, Maggie, one of the scouts said that he had seen you with two braves, one with only one arm and the other a kid."

"They left because they knew you would accuse them of killing your soldiers."

"I don't see how a cripple and a boy could have overpowered my men. All of the tracks went south. My orders were to find the deserters, and I did that, but I'll follow the Indians' trail a ways and make sure they did not double back. Where are you going, Maggie?"

"We are going to Fort Dodge to trade for supplies. Then I need to help these people return to their tribe. After that, I want to find some good land and raise chickens, hogs, and cattle."

"That's crazy, Maggie. Don't you realize how dangerous it is out here, and don't you know there is a bounty on Indian scalps? The bounty is supposed to be only for braves, but the bureaucrats can't tell the difference between male and female scalps or how old they are. You need to just send these sava—people on their way, sell everything you have, and head back to Topeka. This is no place for a woman on her own. You need to come with me now."

"First, Captain Evens, I am perfectly capable of taking care of myself. Second, I will not abandon these women and children. What would you and your men have done to them had I not been here? Whose brilliant idea was it to put a bounty on scalps?"

"Maggie, you're a stubborn woman. I won't be responsible for your safety."

"Oh please! I did not ask for your help. Just leave us alone, and take your fine, upstanding examples of manhood with you."

Evens started to walk away but then turned back. "If you ever find their tribe, Maggie, I don't think the braves will treat you near as well as your own kind."

When Snow finished, we were all very quiet. Maggie had gone to tend to the horses and was now returning. Her eyes were red; she had obviously been crying. Sunrise had fallen asleep, still clutching her doll to her chest with her light-brown curly hair falling part way over her face. Holding her in my arms gave me peace. Snow Flower sat quietly smiling. Sometimes I go back to that place and time.

Short Feather's drumming became softer and softer, and eventually stopped. He had gone back to that place and time. He was smiling.

13

> "We know little about a person until their
> character is revealed by their actions.
> Then we see a friend or an enemy."
>
> —Short Feather

Short Feather was quiet for ten or fifteen minutes. Juanita, still holding Lee's hand, put her other hand on his arm and her head on his shoulder, and closed her eyes. The smell of Juanita's hair was intoxicating, and Lee closed his eyes as well.

"What a beautiful picture you two make," said Short Feather. "I wish I had my camera."

Lee and Juanita sat up straight but still held hands. Short Feather closed his eyes and began softly drumming.

We traveled for many days and saw no one, Indian or white. Storm continued to school me in the "art of battle," as he called it, and Maggie, Snow, Storm, and I continued working on languages. Little Sunrise and Rain Catcher also began learning English and laughed when Maggie struggled with some Cheyenne pronunciations. The other two children were withdrawn and quiet, clinging to their mothers. These were good days, but there was always the underlying fear and tension. Storm and I never slept at the same time and never for more than four hours.

In the evenings, I began making this drum. The snakeskin was perfect for decoration, and Snow gave me a piece of buffalo hide for the drumhead. Little Sunrise would sit quietly and watch me work. When the drum was finished, she wanted to be the first to try it out. She tapped it softly with her fingers and smiled. That is when I started working on a drum for her. It turned out to be better than this one, and she treasured it as much as her doll.

One day, Storm said he was going to scout ahead. He had seen smoke in some hills. When he left, he said to me, "Short Feather, you must be on constant alert." Looking at my rifle, he added, "It is good that you have learned to keep that with you at all times. Remember all that I have taught you."

We had been working with Rain Catcher, teaching him how to read tracks and listen for danger before it could be seen. He became my constant companion and never slept when I did, waking me only once when a bear came too close. Rain Catcher knew it was there before the horses. They are usually the first to know. I was very impressed with him and gave him the bearskin. I was even more impressed when he gave it to Snow, who made a coat for herself and one for Sunrise. Rain Catcher beamed when they wore their coats.

Bruno was also a big help even though he was always close to Sunrise. We decided that he had made himself her guardian.

Maggie was a constant and hard worker. She never seemed to tire, and became the mother of our group. The other women and children always came first, and they continued to regain their health. Maggie was happiest when she would read to us from her book. It had some good stories that she would read in English and then try to tell us in Cheyenne. We all laughed when she said that a man named Moses had turned a walking stick into a snake. Thinking she had used the wrong Cheyenne words, it took us a while to realize that she had chosen correctly.

I tried to help Maggie as much as I could. I loved being with her.

Storm returned to us after four days. He said he had found an Arapaho village and they had told him of a Cheyenne village farther to the north in a valley between two mountains. On his way back, Storm ran into a Cheyenne hunting party, and one of the braves, Deer Slayer, had agreed to guide us to the village.

We were all happy to see Storm, and Sage Woman stared at Deer Slayer. Then she cried out his name and ran to him. He was her dead husband's brother and Rain Catcher's uncle. It had been four winters since they had seen each other, and it was a sad reunion with many tears. Deer Slayer had lost his wife four moons before. She had been a childhood friend of Sage Woman.

The next day, we headed north, with Deer Slayer leading the way. It was good to have a destination. Maggie seemed a little apprehensive although she should not have been. After two more weeks of slow travel, we reached the Cheyenne village. Maggie was accepted with love and respect. Our story had reached the village before us, and she was already a heroine. The village was a mixture of Southern and Northern Cheyenne, and they all turned out to welcome us.

When things settled down, Storm and Deer Slayer were taken to a meeting with the war leader, Dove Song, and other men of the village. Almost all the men in this village were Dog Soldiers. Dove Song was the fiercest and most cunning fighter of all. The meeting lasted most of the afternoon and into the evening. By the time they were finished, Maggie, Snow, Rain Catcher, and I had the tepee and tent set up. Maggie wanted Sage Woman, the other three women, and the two little girls to use the tent, but they had already been divided up among families in the village who were anxious to take care of them. Storm, Rain Catcher, and I ended up with the tepee, Snow and Sunrise in the tent with Maggie.

Storm and Deer Slayer returned to tell me that they and the other men wanted me to be a Dog Soldier. All were committed to driving the white soldiers and settlers out of our land. My hate for the whites was growing because of the fight in the gully and our encounter with the four soldiers who wanted to kill us. Also, I continued to hear stories of the atrocities committed against our people, and not knowing what had happened to Peppermint increased my anxiety. I became a Dog Soldier and committed myself to killing or driving out all whites.

"Short Feather, please stop," said Juanita. "I have some questions."
The drumming stopped, and Short Feather opened his eyes.
"You have hardly mentioned your parents and how they died." Then Juanita asked, "Did you not think of them? I would have thought that your hatred would have come from their deaths more than anything else."

Short Feather was quiet for a moment, then said, "I believe the Great Spirit knew I could not handle that and kept it from my memory for a number of years. No, at this time, I did not think much about my parents except for what they had taught me. The memories of Washita came back to me at a critical moment in 1875. But I cannot get ahead of my story."

"What about Maggie?" asked Juanita. "You said you were committed to killing or driving out all whites."

"Maggie was considered to be Cheyenne and a member of the tribe because of her strong, caring, and accepting nature. To the Cheyenne, one's character and actions were far more important than the color of their skin," Short Feather explained. "To me, Maggie was like my mother and my best friend. In the village, she was everyone's Aunt Maggie, a position of honor."

Lee said, "I always thought to become a Dog Soldier you had to go through an elaborate and difficult ceremony to prove you were brave and strong. Did you not have to do that?"

Short Feather became serious. "In those days, any man could be a Dog Soldier. You were either brave, strong, and a fierce fighter, or you died very quickly. If you lived through your first battle, you were qualified."

"But you were only thirteen," said Juanita.

"I had already proven I could kill, and I was still alive."

They were quiet for a few moments.

"Well," said Short Feather, "let's end on that happy note and get some lunch. We can walk to McDonald's if you two don't walk too fast."

As they walked, Lee asked Short Feather, "How long did you stay with the village?"

"We were there two winters, and I went out on many raids," said Short Feather. "We stole many cattle and horses, burned crops, and disrupted communication. Some Sioux had joined us, and we harassed the Long Knives in Southern Kansas. This was mostly in the spring and summer months, which left the winters for us to rest and recover. Maggie continued to teach our family English. She also taught us to read and write. Ciphering was difficult for me, but Storm and Snow became quite good at it. Rain Catcher was not always interested in learning, but all of the adults insisted and he did progress.

"Maggie also began writing Cheyenne words using the English alphabet. She was very good, and we had no trouble understanding. In the early summer of 1872, our valley was no longer safe from the Long Knives. Some scouts had found us, and we were unable to stop them from returning to Fort Dodge. Most of the Dog Soldiers took their families north to join with the Northern Cheyenne and Sioux tribes that were still fighting. A few went south to join the Cheyenne there.

"Maggie, Snow, Sunrise, and I headed back toward Fort Dodge. Storm came too with his new wife, Sage Woman, and his adopted son, Rain Catcher."

At McDonald's, Short Feather ate two cheeseburgers, fries, and a chocolate shake. Lee and Juanita each had a cheeseburger and Coke and split an order of fries. Total cost was $1.55, which Short Feather insisted on paying.

When they arrived back at Short Feather's apartment, they decided to sit outside and enjoy the day, but the smog drove them back inside. The air conditioner helped.

"Why did you go back to Fort Dodge?" asked Juanita.

"To answer that," said Short Feather, "I must continue my story." He took up his drum and closed his eyes.

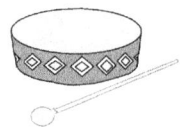

As I told you, we stayed with that village for two winters. During that time, Storm and Sage Woman were married. Rain Catcher was proud to have Storm as his father. They were a very close and loving family.

I learned much from Storm, Dove Song, and the other braves, and found that to be a Dog Soldier was more than being a good fighter. In battle, retreat was never an option, and sometimes, that meant tying ourselves to a picket peg that is beat into the ground. One either fought and prevailed or died. But the most important thing was to prepare both mentally and physically.

I continued to grow and at fifteen was larger than any man in the village. My strength also increased, and soon, I had a following of five young warriors about my age. They made me their leader, and Dove Song often assigned us difficult tasks. We were committed and performed every duty as if the whole world were watching and depending on us. Whether it was carrying water for the village, keeping watch on freezing cold endless nights, or acting as decoys to lure Long Knives into a fight, we never wavered. Thunderstorm remained my mentor, and I had great respect for him even though I now towered over him.

In the spring of 1872, my men and I were seated around a fire listening to Storm. He told us about honor and bravery and that the Great Spirit had created us for an important purpose: to protect and care for the women, children, and old men.

He also said, "We must always consider the welfare of others before thinking of our own wants, needs, and desires. This must be done regardless of the cost, even our own lives."

These were wise words, and I kept them in my heart and mind.

While he talked, I was absentmindedly sharpening a lance I had made.

Snow Flower came and said to her brother, "Storm, six braves have come from the south to join us. One has a bottle of whiskey and is becoming drunk. He is saying things that should not be said."

Storm spoke to Snow, "Perhaps he will pass out. We can take the bottle from him, and I can talk to him in the morning."

Just then we heard a man yelling, "I have heard that the son of the coward Laughing Wolf is here. Where is he? Is he a coward like his father and the other coward Black Kettle?"

A man staggered into the circle. He looked to be about Storm's age, maybe in his late twenties.

Storm recognized him and said, "Yellow Hawk, it is good to see you. Please join us and sit down." He spoke calmly and did not get up.

"I do not want to sit down, Thunderstorm, I want to fight. Where is the son of a coward?" asked Yellow Hawk, spitting out his words.

Yellow Hawk did not see Storm whisper to me, "Be careful, Short Feather, Yellow Hawk is very dangerous, even when drunk, and he is unpredictable." Then Storm said out loud, "Yellow Hawk,

I know this boy. He is no coward, and his father was a brave and good human being."

I sat quietly with my hand on my lance.

Yellow Hawk turned to Storm. "Laughing Wolf would not fight, and followed Black Kettle, who was a coward and a traitor. Black Kettle trusted the white man and led many human beings to their deaths. My wife and two children were murdered at Sand Creek. Laughing Wolf knew the Long Knives would attack and left."

"I have known of your loss and grieve with you," said Storm. "We have all suffered great loss at the hands of the white man."

Yellow Hawk took another drink from his bottle. "I seek satisfaction. Laughing Wolf was a traitor and a coward to follow Black Kettle. Show me his son. I need another scalp to decorate my lodge. Let us all see if the son of a coward will fight and die like a man."

I could take no more, but remained seated. "I am Short Feather, son of Laughing Wolf. I will not fight you. You are drunk. Sleep it off, we can always fight tomorrow."

"So, you are a coward like your father," snarled Yellow Hawk. "You do not deserve to live. I will kill you where you sit."

To everyone's surprise, Yellow Hawk gave a loud war cry and jumped over the fire. With a knife in each hand, he jumped again and flew directly at me.

Instinctively, I raised the tip of my lance with the other end planted firmly on the ground. Yellow Hawk became impaled on my lance through his chest, and died almost instantly.

Everyone was quiet. Snow had her hand over her mouth, as if to stifle a scream.

I got up slowly, saying, "It is late. I think I will sleep now," and walked away. I could hear Storm begin to sing a death song.

The next morning, I woke early and found my friends and Storm at the entrance to my lodge. Some were sleeping, some were standing guard. Yellow Hawk's brother and friends had sworn vengeance. I wondered at this because Yellow Hawk had caused his own death. His drunkenness, impulsiveness, and foolish fighting style defied common sense, and besides, he attacked me.

Storm took me aside and told me that it would probably be best if we left the village. There were many Dog Soldiers that did not understand Black Kettle or anyone who followed him. Yellow Hawk had revived many bad feelings and reminded them that my father did not fight at Sand Creek.

As we were talking, Dove Song came to us, wanting to talk. "I have spoken to Yellow Hawk's brother, Little Hawk. He is three winters younger than Yellow Hawk and has not yet proven himself in battle. His brother was very protective, and always gave him jobs that kept him out of harm's way. Little Hawk is an intelligent and reasonable human being but feels that he must fight you, Short Feather, or he will lose face. He is not a big man, maybe half your size. I fear you must fight him, and if you win, you must leave our village."

"I do not wish to fight Little Hawk," I said. "If we do fight, I will prevail."

Dove Song became thoughtful. "If you do not, you will be branded a coward and Little Hawk will be compelled to hunt you down or be branded a coward. This is not good, and I wish I could resolve it in another way. Little Hawk is waiting in the field where the ponies graze."

When I arrived at the field, there was already a large crowd. Little Hawk was standing about one hundred paces away. He wore nothing from the waist up and had no weapon that I could see. Dove Song was correct; Little Hawk was not a big man. I gave my rifle and six-shooter to Storm, took off my shirt, placed it on the ground, and left my knife there also. This was the first time in two years that I had not had my rifle close at hand. I felt totally naked.

The crowd jeered as I walked to Little Hawk. Just before I got to him, he turned around so that his back was to me and the spectators. I had to walk around him, and I stood about three feet away. He walked up to me so that we were only about three inches apart. I had to look down to see his face; he had to look up. I could see tears on Little Hawk's face.

"Short Feather, I must tell you about my brother. He has been trying since Sand Creek to get himself killed in battle. He finally did it, and unfortunately, we are victims also. We must fight, but I do not wish to harm you. I will do all that I can to win, or I will never be respected as a Dog Soldier." Little Hawk said these things with his fists clenched and his body rigid, as if he were taunting me.

I assumed the same posture. I said, "I also do not wish to harm you, my friend, but we will have to make this look real, and there must be blood."

Little Hawk almost smiled. "Be sure to hit me in the nose. You will not have to hit very hard, it bleeds easily."

"Come at me furiously and fast, I will be slow." Then I said, "You are a good man, Little Hawk. You will always have my respect. Now, let us give them a good show."

Little Hawk turned his back to me, walked about ten paces, and turned to face me. He gave a loud war cry and charged. I was surprised by his speed and the power with which he hit me. We went down in a cloud of dust, and he began pummeling my face with his fists. I threw him off, and he landed about ten paces away. There were groans from the crowd.

Just as I got up, he was already at me again. We rolled and punched, throwing up much dirt and grass. Then we stood to face each other again, and he kicked me in the groin. This was not at all pleasant, so I punched him in the nose. He was right about his nose because now there was blood everywhere, with more groans from the crowd. We punched and wrestled for what seemed to be a very long time, and then, when he was choking me, he whispered, spitting blood, "Short Feather, I grow tired. We need to end this."

I said, "Me too, I will throw you off again. Come at me and punch me in the nose. I will go down and not get up."

Little Hawk did as I said, but he hit me so hard I did not want to get up. Now there was blood all over me too. There were cheers from the crowd as Little Hawk stood over me and said loud enough for all to hear, "Short Feather, you fought bravely. I will not kill you."

Soon, I was laying alone in the field with only Storm standing over me. He shook his head and said, "Short Feather, never in my life have I ever seen such a fierce fake fight. I think you convinced everyone but me. I could not be more proud of you."

14

> "Why do we know so little of each other?
> Perhaps it is time to learn to listen."
>
> —Lee Grant

Maggie and Snow came to see what the damage was and to help me get back to my lodge. Neither said anything. They just looked at me like I was an errant child.

After I got cleaned up, Dove Song came to us and said that most were satisfied, but two of Yellow Hawk's friends still wanted me dead. He also told us some Crow scouts had been seen and they had to have seen our village, so it was time to move on. Most of the Dog Soldiers were going to go north to join our brothers who were fighting there with the Sioux against the Long Knives. The rest were heading south to join with the Comanche.

I was now a leader without any followers. All my men decided to join Little Hawk. He was now greatly respected since he had beaten a known warrior twice his size in hand-to-hand combat. I did not see him again for three years.

The fact that I still knew nothing of what had happened to Peppermint was weighing heavily on me. There had been little I could do before, but now I believed I could start my search for her. My English was good, thanks to Maggie. Storm had taught me not only how to fight but also how to be an actor. I decided it was time to go to work for the Long Knives to try and get information about the Washita captives. In this way, I felt that maybe, just maybe, I could learn what had happened to my sister. The most logical place to start was Fort Dodge.

Maggie agreed and said she needed to check on her finances, and thought she might be able to do that at Fort Dodge. She and her husband had left all their savings in a Topeka bank. More importantly, however, was that she felt she was in a better position to get information about Peppermint.

Storm, with his wife, Sage Woman, and son, Rain Catcher, decided to come with us. Storm said that our whole group made a great team, and he saw no reason to break it up. Snow and Maggie had become very close and were dependent on each other. I was happy that Snow would stay with us because Sunrise, now five years old, had become my little sister. I could not imagine being separated from her.

We were the last to leave the valley. We now had more horses, oxen, cattle, and chickens. Maggie's chicken population had grown substantially over two years. She gave many away to other families, keeping only the number that we could handle on our trip. In return, she was given moccasins and other items of clothing. It was sad to leave the valley, and Maggie said she would like to return someday to build her ranch. At this time, it was not safe, and we had other things to do.

Short Feather stopped drumming and opened his eyes. "I think it is time for me to take a break," he said, as he got up.

When the bathroom door closed, Lee looked at Juanita and spoke softly, "What an amazing story, and what a privilege it is to hear it."

"I have known Short Feather now for over three years," responded Juanita. "I always just thought of him as a feisty, sweet but lonely old man. Now I see a completely different person. It is sad that we know so little of those who have gone before us. Older people have so much to give, but today, we just see them as a hindrance."

"I know what you mean," said Lee. "I realize now that I know little about my parents. They are going to have to sit down and answer all of my questions."

The toilet flushed, but Short Feather did not come out.

After a few more minutes, Lee went to the door. "Sir, are you all right?"

Short Feather opened the door, went to his chair, and sat down. "Yes, I am fine. It appears, White Tears, that I am going to have to put up with you fussing over me as well as Buffa—Juanita. I was just looking in the mirror and saw an old man. My mind thinks I am still young, but the mirror and my body tell the truth. I don't know how much longer I have on this earth, but why do I have to spend my last days being pestered by you two?"

"We are concerned for you," said Juanita. "And besides, you have to stay around long enough to finish your story, old man. I want to know the rest."

"Sometimes you're a pain, Juanita," said Short Feather with a smile. "Speaking of a pain, can you two be here next Saturday? My great-grandson is coming, and I want you to meet him. He is a very successful attorney and handles all of my affairs. I don't think he knows that he is an Indian, much less Cheyenne, but he means well. I call him Tornado. You will know why when you meet him."

"I'll be here," said Lee.

"I will be too," said Juanita. "And I will be here to check up on you and clean on my regular days. What time do you want us, and will there be time for you to tell us more of your story? Life is short."

"Come whenever you want, but next time, bring only chocolate doughnuts."

Lee and Juanita laughed.

"I'm serious," said Short Feather. "Chocolate is health food—mental health. And yes, I will tell you more. Tornado will not take up too much time."

"I'll bring lunch," announced Juanita. "You were very slow going to McDonald's. For a while there, I thought Lee was going to have to carry you, you old Indian."

"Be careful, I may start calling you by your Indian name just to make you go away, you little Mexican." Short Feather pretended to be irritated.

"Now, you two children stop picking on each other," interrupted Lee. "There is time for you to tell us more, Short Feather, so take up your drum, close your eyes, and please get on with it."

Juanita stuck her tongue out at Short Feather. He blew her a kiss and picked up his drum.

"Grandfather," said Lee, "before you go on, may I ask you a question?"

"You have just given me a wonderful compliment, White Tears, by addressing me as Grandfather. Of course, you may ask anything," said Short Feather with obvious emotion.

"Why did you name Juanita Buffalo Tail?"

"If I tell you, Juanita will no longer resent it, and that will deprive me of much fun," said Short Feather with a sly grin. "When I named her that, I did not know how much fun it would be."

"Now you must tell us, Grandfather," said Juanita. "If you do not, I will be angry, and that will definitely *not* be fun."

"Okay, okay," said Short Feather, and he began speaking slowly. "I will tell you. When I was young, my mother, Buffalo Woman, and my sister, Peppermint, would fix their hair in two long braids. They would attach a buffalo tail decorated with beads to their right braid as an ornament. Whenever I see them in my mind, they have that buffalo tail in their hair, and it brings wonderful emotions and beautiful feelings. The first time I ever saw you, my little Buffalo Tail, you gave me those same feelings."

Juanita was very touched.

Short Feather got up and went to his bedroom. He came back with a small wooden box and sat in his chair. He took two buffalo tails out of the box and set the box aside. The tails were beautifully decorated with beads of different colors near the top, and just below the beads there was a ring of braided leather. On one, the leather ring was dyed blue; on the other, it was red.

Short Feather handed the one with blue leather to Juanita. "This is for you. It was made and given to me by Sage Woman and is from the first buffalo I shot. It is the buffalo that fed the starving women and children in the gully. I will always be grateful to the Great Spirit and the spirit of the buffalo."

He became quiet, and said almost in a whisper as he caressed the buffalo tail with red, "This one belonged to my wife. It would not be appropriate for me to give it to you."

Short Feather closed his eyes and went to another place.

After about ten minutes, the phone rang. Short Feather opened his eyes and answered.

"Hello? Yes, I remember, how are you? That would be very nice. They are here now, let me ask." Short Feather held the phone to his chest. "This is Healing Breeze, Dr. Bronson. We met him and his wife at Puddingstone Lake. They have invited us to dinner next Saturday. They want to hear more of my story. Would you two like to come?"

"Yes, we would," said Lee and Juanita at the same time.

"Yes, Dr. Bronson, we would be honored. Okay, Healing Breeze it is. I think I can do that. About 1:00 p.m., you say? Sure, is there anything we can bring? Okay, we will be looking forward to it."

Short Feather turned to Lee and Juanita. "Healing Breeze said that dinner would be at six, but he wants to pick me up at one o'clock to catch them up on what I have told you two. He said you could come then also, if you want. What do you think?"

Lee started to say yes, but Juanita stopped him. "We will be there at five. Do you still want us to meet your grandson?"

"Yes, Tornado will be here about 10:00 a.m. Why don't you two come about 9:30?"

"Is that okay with you, Juanita?" asked Lee.

"Yes, that will be fine," said Juanita. She seemed to be in deep thought about something else.

Lee said, "Then it is settled. We'll be here at nine thirty on Saturday, but we must go now. It is almost five, and we have taken up your whole day."

Juanita gave Short Feather a long hug and a kiss on the cheek. She was holding the buffalo tail like it was a precious diamond.

15

> "Money can corrupt and do terrible things. It can also do much good. Money is not the root of all evil. Read it again."
>
> —Short Feather

Lee took Juanita out to dinner at his favorite steak house. The food was wonderful, and the restaurant was usually quiet. Lee ordered a porterhouse steak with baked potato and vegetables. Juanita ordered a petite filet mignon with broccoli only.

While they were waiting for their order, Lee asked, "Juanita, when did your family come to this country?"

Juanita took a sip of water and smiled sweetly. "My family was living here before 'here' was part of this country."

"I don't understand," said Lee, stammering a little.

Juanita spoke quietly. "My ancestors came from Mexico to the Pomona Valley around 1830. They settled the land after the Indians were wiped out by the diseases brought in with the missions. Then white settlers took most of the land from us, and we became part of the United States. My family has been here for nine generations."

"I had no idea," said Lee. "I am ashamed that I know so little of the history of this area. We visited missions when I was a kid in school, but I paid little attention."

Juanita, just barely speaking above a whisper, said, "I am ashamed that what I have told you just now is all I know of the history of my family."

Lee asked, "What about your parents?"

"My father inherited the house where I live with Jose and Maria. My grandfather built the house on a small piece of land that he inherited from his father. Father was a plumber and a very good one. He was in high demand and made good money, saving and investing most of it. He was thrifty and strict. He died at the age of thirty-six. Mother said he had a bad heart but never knew it. Mother died four years ago. She was only forty-seven. Father's investments supported us but were pretty much gone by the time mother died. Jose got his job at the phone company, and I started my cleaning business."

"What about college?" asked Lee.

Juanita looked a little sad. "I would love to go to college. My grade average was 4.0 in high school. I always got straight As. But college is not going to happen. No money."

"What would you want to study?"

"Some field of medicine, perhaps nursing. I think I would make a good nurse," answered Juanita.

"I think you would be a fantastic nurse," said Lee.

Their food was served, and they enjoyed a wonderful meal together.

The next Saturday morning, Lee and Juanita arrived at Short Feather's at exactly nine thirty. They brought chocolate-frosted doughnuts, and Short Feather immediately took one. Lee and Short Feather talked about politics and the Vietnam War, which had now become a full-blown war. Juanita sat quietly.

"White Tears, I am afraid we are boring Buffalo Tail," said Short Feather. "I do have something else that I want to talk about before Tornado gets here. What are your plans for your education?"

Lee was taken by surprise, but answered, "I just got my liberal arts degree from the junior college, and I have been accepted at Cal

Poly. I start there in the fall. I have saved up enough money, and with the GI bill, I will be able to devote most of my time to school. I will be working part-time."

"That sounds good," said Short Feather. "What about you, Juanita?"

"You and my other customers keep me way too busy. I have no plans," said Juanita, as she got up to get the coffee she had started earlier.

Edward Conrad—attorney-at-law, Short Feather's great-grandson—walked in without knocking. He was a very good-looking middle-aged man wearing an expensive suit. About five feet ten, he dominated the room, having an air of authority and impatience and also friendliness.

"Grandfather, I do not have much time. Is Miss Trujio here?" asked Edward.

Short Feather frowned. "Tornado, you are early. I have not told her yet, and I am going to use the bathroom. Please sit down."

Lee was already standing, and introduced himself. "My name is Lee Grant."

"Edward Conrad. Glad to meet you."

They shook hands and sat down—Lee on the couch, Edward on a hard-back chair.

"May I ask what is going on?" said Lee.

"No, this is Grandfather's party. We will have to wait for him," answered Edward.

Juanita brought in the coffee, and introductions were made.

"Short Feather is a remarkable man," said Lee.

Edward had just taken a bite of a doughnut, and almost choked. "*Remarkable* is an understatement, but I would have to throw in *stubborn*, *difficult*, *unreasonable*, *unpredictable*, and *brilliant*. I am about the only family he has left. You should also know that he is doing quite well financially. He owns this apartment building and two others. The others are much nicer. I don't know why he chooses to live here."

"The people, Tornado, it's the people," said Short Feather as he came back and sat down. "And you talk too much."

"Maybe so," said Edward. "But we both know you were going to tell them, anyway."

"Okay," said Short Feather. "Since Tornado is in such a hurry, let's get on with it. Lee, Juanita, three weeks ago, I decided it was time to die. Telling you two my story has caused me to want to live a little longer."

"Well, I am glad to hear that, old man," said Juanita. "I can't afford to lose a customer."

Short Feather laughed.

"Can we please get to my part?" said Edward impatiently.

"Yes, of course," said Short Feather. "Juanita, I have spoken to your brother, Jose. He told me that you have been very sad that you have not been able to go to college. It would be my privilege to finance your education."

Juanita's mouth dropped open, and she gasped.

"Okay, here is where I come in," said Edward. "I am an alumnus of USC and am on the board of directors. I also have friends in high places at other colleges and universities. With your grades and my contacts, you can go just about anywhere you want. Yes, I checked on your grades in high school. You will submit all bills for tuition, books, etc., to my office, and they will be paid from a trust that I have set up for Grandfather. You will also receive $400 per month starting this month, and until you are finished with school and gainfully employed. Here is my card. You will be working mainly with my secretary, Sylvia. Any questions?"

Juanita was in shock. After a few moments, she got up, went to Short Feather, and hugged him around the neck for a very long time.

"I'll take that as a no," said Edward as he looked at Lee. "Mr. Grant, I have also been instructed to tell you to submit any education bills that are not covered by the GI bill. Nice to meet you, here is my card. Please call Sylvia. She will take care of the details for you and Miss Trujio."

Edward Conrad, attorney-at-law, left as quickly as he had come—like a tornado.

Lee almost fell back on the couch. Juanita finally let go of Short Feather, because he said he could not breathe. She stayed seated on the armrest with her arm across his shoulders. Lee and Juanita just looked at each other.

Short Feather finally spoke up. "I thought you said you were going to bring lunch, Buffalo Tail."

"Oh, my goodness, I forgot," cried Juanita. "I made enchiladas and left them in the fridge at home."

Short Feather laughed. "That's okay. We are going to have a big dinner tonight with the Bronsons. I'll just have another doughnut now and some cheese and crackers for lunch. You two run along. I am sure you have things to talk about, and I need a nap before Healing Breeze picks me up."

Lee took Juanita directly home. She said she had much to do before he picked her up at four thirty. Then she said, "Why don't you come at four? Jose wants to talk to you."

16

> "Sometimes it is best to take a deep
> breath and admire pure beauty."
>
> —Short Feather

Jose offered Lee a Coke, and they sat in the living room.

"I asked you to come early because I need to talk to you about the old Indian," said Jose. "His attorney came by last week and made me an offer on this house. He said it would make a good rental."

Lee took a drink of his Coke. "Everything is sure happening fast, Joe. It is hard to take it all in. I only met Edward Conrad this morning. Is it a good offer?"

Jose laughed a little. "He offered my asking price in cash. I set it high because I knew I would have to come down. If this is real, Maria and Juanita will be very happy. I have an appointment with him on Tuesday. Why don't you come too?"

"Yes, I will, and has Juanita told you about our meeting this morning?" asked Lee.

"All she said was that she was going to go to college. Then she grabbed Maria, and they dragged out all of Mother's old clothes. They have been in Juanita's room all afternoon. Sometimes I hear them giggling and laughing. Juanita has been acting strangely lately. What have you and that old Indian done to her?"

"Joe, I don't know what we may have done to her, but I know what she has done to me," said Lee while looking at his hands. "I realize that we only met three weeks ago, but I believe that I love her."

"Lee," said Jose after a few quiet moments. "I have heard that said by a number of other men. It is easy to fall in love with Juanita. She turned them all down, so don't get your hopes up. She has not been her usual self, however, since she met you."

Maria walked into the room. She was holding the baby, and had a big smile. She looked down the hall toward Juanita's room.

Juanita walked into the living room. When Lee saw Juanita, he found he was having difficulty breathing. Jose just stared with his mouth wide open. Lee stood up but felt weak all over.

Juanita was wearing a beautiful traditional fiesta ensemble with a white cotton blouse that rested just below her shoulders. The top of the blouse was ruffled with red, blue, and yellow flowers as well as some green leaves, all hand embroidered. Her skirt was black, with four bands of embroidered flowers about an inch apart around the skirt above the hemline, which reached to her ankles. With a red sash tied at her waist, she was the ideal Mexican senorita.

The most remarkable features that stood out to her three observers, however, were her hair and face. Juanita's long shiny black hair was parted down the middle with two braids that reached halfway down her back. Woven into each braid was a blue-and-red ribbon. Attached to her right braid was the buffalo tail that Short Feather had given her. The only makeup she wore was a little lipstick. Her skin glowed like a beautiful sunset, the color of amber.

Juanita turned a complete circle on her black pumps and, with her eyes sparkling, asked, "Well, what do you think?"

Maria just cried.

Jose said, "Mother made that outfit. If she were here now, she would be crying like Maria. You look amazing."

Lee walked to Juanita and took her hands. "Never in my life have I seen anyone or, for that matter, anything more beautiful than you. I just hope that Short Feather has a strong heart, because mine almost stopped."

Juanita blushed, rose up on her toes, and kissed Lee on the cheek.

17

> "Acting is the ability to become someone
> that one is not. Deception? Maybe.
> Necessary? Often."
>
> —Short Feather

Dr. Jacob Bronson, his wife, Allison, and their baby daughter, Clara Lee, lived in a beautiful home in Diamond Bar, a new community in the hills southwest of Pomona. Lee and Juanita arrived at exactly 5:00 p.m. The doctor went out to greet them and show them in. Allison met them at the door, and put her index finger to her lips. They walked quietly to the family room, where Short Feather was lying on his back on the couch, sound asleep. Clara Lee was on his chest, also sound asleep. His big hands were gently on her back.

The Bronsons showed Lee and Juanita to the living room where Allison said quietly, "Let's let them sleep a little longer. I think we wore poor Short Feather out, and little Breeze has fallen in love with him."

Then, looking at Juanita, she said, "Juanita, you are beautiful and so radiant."

"Yes," said the doctor. "Breathtakingly beautiful. I feel honored that you have come to our home. Lee, I hope that you will not let her get away."

This time, both Lee and Juanita blushed.

Allison asked, "Is that the buffalo tail that Short Feather told us about?"

"Yes, it is," said Juanita. "I wanted to wear it for him."

"It is so beautiful because of what it stands for. He will be so pleased," said Allison. "Whenever he speaks of you, I can tell he loves you very much."

"You called the baby Breeze," said Juanita questioningly.

"We fell in love with that name because that is what she has been in our lives—a soft, warm breeze," said Jacob. "We are changing her name to Breeze Claralee."

They could hear the baby fussing. Allison went to the family room and returned with a sleepy-eyed but happy little girl.

"Short Feather will be out shortly," said Allison. "He wanted to wash his face."

They could hear Short Feather walking slowly down the hallway. As he approached, he was looking down, measuring his steps, and placing his canes so that he did not hit anything. Juanita stood and he stopped.

Short Feather looked up and into her eyes. Taking a deep breath and letting it out slowly, his tears began to fall.

The room was totally silent.

Finally, Short Feather said, "If I lived another hundred years, I would not expect to see a more lovely vision of pure beauty."

Jacob said a quiet "Amen."

Short Feather seemed a little unsteady, so Lee and Jacob helped him to a big leather recliner. He could not take his eyes off Juanita. She began to feel uncomfortable, so she sat down.

Breeze put out her hand toward Short Feather and cooed. Allison placed her on his lap.

There was a professional-looking camera on the coffee table. Allison picked it up and said, "I hope all of you will let me take pictures."

"Allison is a wonder at photography," said Jacob. "She has a way of capturing just the right angles and light and has had some of her pictures appear in magazines."

Allison proceeded to take six pictures of Short Feather and Breeze. Then she looked at Juanita.

A short, squat, white middle-aged woman with the bearing of a military general came out of the kitchen and looked at all of them appraisingly. Wonderful smells followed her.

"Dinner will be ready in twenty minutes," was all she said. She turned and went back to the kitchen.

Lee and Juanita looked at Allison.

Allison was slightly embarrassed. "After we invited all of you to dinner, I remembered that I am a terrible cook. I hired Mrs. Bancroft for the evening. She can make a TV dinner into a gourmet meal."

For the next twenty minutes, Allison used up the roll of film in her camera and another roll taking pictures of Juanita from every angle and with every background that she could think of.

Dinner was amazing. Beef Wellington, with boiled white potatoes and asparagus cooked to perfection, was the main course after a wonderful salad; for dessert, crème brûlée. When Mrs. Bancroft came into the dining room to pick up the dessert dishes, every one stood and applauded. She turned very red, said, "Oh my," and went back to the kitchen.

After dinner, with Breeze in her crib for the night, everyone wanted Short Feather to tell more of his story.

"I believe I have all of you to the early summer of 1872, when I am sixteen years old and we are traveling to Fort Dodge," said Short Feather as he took his drum from its bag. He closed his eyes and began drumming softly.

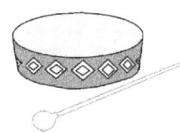

We were a close family with Maggie, Snow Flower, Sunrise, Thunderstorm, Sage Woman, Rain Catcher, myself, and, of course, Bruno. Travel was slow because of our mobile farm. In the evenings, Maggie would read from her book and talk about a man named Jesus. She said He is the Son of God and that He was killed, but she talked about Him like He is alive.

I began to like hearing about this Jesus. The other adults would tell stories that they had learned as children. It was a special time, and our love for each other grew.

The worst part of our travels was the awful smell of dead animals that sometimes came our way. Every day we could hear gunfire. Sometimes close, sometimes it was far away. We passed fields of slaughter where hundreds of buffalo had been shot with the meat left to rot. We could not understand this wasteful killing. It is estimated that during the years 1872 and 1873, five thousand buffalo were killed each and every day. I later learned that the killing of the buffalo was part of the strategy to destroy the Indian nations and our way of life.

We did manage to collect a good number of buffalo hides that Storm said we would be able to sell. It also turned out that there was a market for bones, horns, and skulls.

We reached the Fort Dodge area in the fall of 1872 and set up camp on the south side of the Arkansas River, about five miles west of the fort. The next day, we discovered that a town had been staked out on the north side of the river about a mile from where we were camped. It was being called Dodge City. The railroad had already come through and gone beyond.

In order to be perceived as less of a threat in white society and to the army, I began to play the part of a big stupid Indian. Maggie and I went to Fort Dodge. I was wearing John Lawson's clothes, which fit pretty well except that the pant legs were too short. This, however, aided my act. Maggie went directly to the fort commander. When Maggie came out, she grabbed my shirtsleeve and hauled me toward the stables. There was an officer standing outside.

"Lieutenant Hays?" asked Maggie.

"Yes, ma'am," said the officer.

"Major Porter says that you are to put this big stupid Indian to work in your stable. He understands just enough English for you to tell him what to do. He is very strong, a good worker, animals love him, and he will not give you any trouble. His name is Ken, and—this is very important—do not let him have any money. He would not know what to do with it, so any wage he earns shall be delivered to me, and I know what the wage is to be. Am I making myself clear?" Maggie came across so forcefully I don't think I would have wanted to argue with her. Storm had been a good acting teacher for both of us.

The lieutenant nodded yes, and Maggie left. Lieutenant Hays walked around, looking me over. I just stared at the ground.

"Why me?" asked Hays of no one. He then yelled at a man cleaning stalls inside the stable, "Private, get out here." When the private arrived, Hays said, "Put this Injun to work. If he causes any trouble, I'll hold you responsible."

Still looking at the ground, I said, "Ken good Injun."

"Yeah, sure, I've heard that one before," said Private Jim Cable as he pushed me toward the stable.

That is when I began my career working for the US Army. I was good with animals and did work hard. So much so that soon, Jim and the other private had little to do. They loved the fact that whatever they told me to do, I did quickly and well.

Many nights I would sleep in the stable. The privates had quarters at one end, and I had no problem listening to their conversations. In fact, I became quite good at listening to conversations all over the fort, but no one ever talked about Washita.

I worked at the fort throughout the winter, traveling back to Maggie and the others as often as I could. Maggie's money was in a bank in Topeka. She transferred all of it to the new bank in

Dodge City. Using some of the money, she and Snow opened a mercantile store.

With the railroad and cattle drives coming through, business was good. Storm and Rain Catcher would make trips to where the buffalo had been killed and bring back more bones, skulls, and hooves. Sometimes they would find new kills and bring back buffalo hides. Sage Woman made Indian artifacts from the buffalo parts. These sold really well to the tourists and travelers who came through on the trains. When I visited, I was amazed to see how well they had progressed.

Maggie was always talking to soldiers and former soldiers about Washita. She would ask innocent questions, trying to get them to talk about the women and children who were taken. Whenever she got close to that subject, the men would either clam up or claim they knew nothing about it.

One corporal, who was slightly drunk, did say, "Yeah, I was there. Them squaws was fer officers only. When we had to move out, they had ta jus let 'em go 'cause they couldn't take 'em with us."

Maggie asked, "One of the little girls was named Peppermint. She was ten years old and was very outgoing. Do you remember a little girl like that?"

"Sure do," said the corporal. "Didn't know her name, but the actor took her away after what she done to the Crow scout what tried to have his way with her. Gutted him like a deer."

"Actor?" questioned Maggie as she worked hard to control her emotions.

"Said he and his girls were there to entertain the troops, and actually, they weren't bad. Did funny skits, and they sung good. Da girls weren't bad to look at."

"Do you remember his name?" asked Maggie.

"Nope," said the soldier as he walked away.

That was our first clue about Peppermint. It wasn't much, but at least it was something.

When the weather got really cold, the stable privates said I could sleep in their quarters by the stove. They became protective of me because I did all the work, and all they had to do was play cards and watch for the lieutenant, who seldom visited. When he did, they would always be hard at work.

One night, while they were playing cards, Jim asked, "Ken, where you from, and how did ya git under the thumb of that Maggie?"

I pretended to be confused and said, "Maggie find Ken by Washita. Ken hurt bad in head, you want see scar?"

"No," said Jim. "I've seen enough scars. You were at Washita?"

"Washita bad place. Mother and Father killed. Ken shot in head. Ken see sister taken in wagon. Ken miss sister." I said this while watching their faces with a dumb look on my face.

Jim's face changed color, and he looked away. The other private did not react.

"Jim know 'bout Washita?" I asked.

Jim cleared his throat. "I was there, damn waste kill'n all them ponies. Wha'd yer sister look like? I drove one of them wagons."

"Ken's sister only ten winters old. She have long hair and very pretty. Ken wants to know where sister is, really bad."

"There was one little girl I remember," said Jim. "Actually, she was hard to forget, spunky little thing. The squaws was divided up to the officers at Camp Supply, but the general said to leave the kids alone. One of the Crows decided he didn't have to follow that order and went after that little girl. He got sliced from navel to chin, I understand. An actor took that little girl with him when he left 'cause the Crow were not happy that one of their own was kilt by a little Cheyenne girl."

"What is *actor*?" I asked.

"Someone who pretends to be something he is not," said Jim. "This guy was not bad. He sung pretty good and did a comedy bit with the two girls he had with him. We figured out that the girls were his daughters. They had real nice voices too."

"Jim know actor's name?" I asked.

"Clive Cornelius, or something like that, but he's long gone. Headed back east, I hear tell."

In the early spring, Maggie came and got me. She told the soldiers she needed me in Dodge City because her business was growing. Maggie and I figured I had learned all that I could at Fort Dodge. Jim was very upset when I left. He had to go back to work.

It was good to be home and spend more time with Sunrise and Rain Catcher. All of us now wore white man's clothes except for when the trains came through. Storm had constructed a booth at the train depot where we sold the "Original Indian Artifacts" Sage Woman, Sunrise, and Rain Catcher made. They were getting good at it, and Sunrise could sell anything to the travelers when she was dressed in her Cheyenne clothes and batted her eyes.

Maggie's and Snow's store was also becoming popular because of the high quality of everything they sold, and people really liked them. They had already made two trips to Kansas City to buy merchandise and were very good at bargaining for good prices.

Storm was becoming quite the entrepreneur also. His name was now Jonathan T. Storm, Esquire. He dressed the part while in town, wearing tan trousers with suspenders, a striped shirt, a fashionable tie, and a single-breasted frock coat. His shoes were always shiny. How he managed that in Dodge City, I could never figure out. He even cut his hair, and would have passed for white if it had not been for his dark skin and sharp Cheyenne facial features. His English was so good, however, that he easily fit in with most whites.

One day, just after I returned home, a tall well-dressed man arrived on the train. He said he was from New York City and offered to buy all the original Indian artifacts Storm and Sage Woman had. Saying they would sell well back east, he paid the same prices that they were being sold for one at a time. The man also said that he would be back in ninety days and hoped that they would have more to sell.

Because of this, Storm and I started traveling to collect whatever we thought would sell. One of our first stops was Camp Supply in Oklahoma. No one there seemed to know anything about the Washita captives. The Indian agency for that area was now located there, and we were able to trade on the reservation. It was sad to see the poor condition of our brothers and sisters. Most were happy to accept our money for their handcrafted items.

On one trip, more to the north and west, we came across another buffalo killing field. This time, we had Rain Catcher with us. We set about to collect as many buffalo hides as we could and had been working hard for most of the day.

All of a sudden, Rain Catcher yelled "Hunter!" just as a bullet passed through Storm's empty sleeve. If his arm had been there, it would have been blown off.

We sought cover as fast as we could, and there were three more shots fired. Rain Catcher was hiding behind a dead buffalo and could not move or he would have been in the open. I found myself in the same predicament hiding behind a boulder. I did have my rifle but had no idea where the hunter was.

Then I saw Storm run toward a shallow gully. He ran fast, and when a bullet raised the dust behind him, he ran even faster. Everything was quiet for a while, and I decided to put my hat on a stick and raise it up. This was not a smart thing to do because I now had a bullet hole in my almost-new hat. After a while, we heard more gunshots, but these sounded like they were from a six-shooter.

Then we heard Storm yelling for us, and I looked up over my boulder to see him standing up and waving his arm. He was on a rise a long ways off. Rain Catcher and I took our horses and rode to Storm. When we got there, we saw Storm was standing over a dead white man.

"His horses are over there," said Storm, pointing to his right with the hunter's rifle. "He won't need them anymore. Looks like he was out here on his own."

We collected the horses—one a packhorse—and two more buffalo hides. Then we headed toward Dodge City. It was about four days away.

The second day, we came across a small Cheyenne village and traded the hunter's rifle, horses, and supplies for six deer hides and four pairs of beautifully made moccasins. They were every bit as good as the ones Sage Woman made. Storm also bargained for a buckskin dress that was decorated with beads and brightly colored feathers.

As we were getting ready to leave, Storm took one of our buffalo hides, as a bonus, and gave it to the woman who had made the dress.

Short Feather stopped and opened his eyes. We all heard Breeze fussing in the nursery. Allison went to check on her and came back carrying a happy, wide-awake little Breeze. Juanita asked if she could hold her. The baby seemed happy to be back with the adults, and wanted to touch all the flowers embroidered on Juanita's blouse.

Mrs. Bancroft brought in a tray with coffee and another with water and glasses. She said she was finished cleaning up and would be on her way. Jacob walked her home. Her house was only three houses away.

Allison took a few pictures of Juanita and Breeze.

Lee said to Short Feather, "You said that Rain Catcher yelled, 'Hunter,' just as the first shot was fired. How did he know the hunter was there?"

"I asked the same question," said Short Feather. "Rain Catcher said he did not know how he knew. He just knew."

When Jacob returned, he said, "Grandfather, you speak of your time at Fort Dodge casually, as if you were accepting the white world. Storm seemed to fit right in and adapted quite well. How do you explain this?"

Short Feather was quiet for a few minutes. "I was at Fort Dodge for one reason and one reason only: to try and get information about Peppermint. If I thought it would have helped find her, I would have killed every man there without giving it a second's thought, starting with Private Jim Cable. I was sixteen years old, and my hate ran deep."

"What about Storm?" asked Lee.

"Storm was the most pragmatic man I have ever known. He killed the buffalo hunter because the hunter was trying to kill him. He adapted to and accepted the white world because he realized that was the only way he and his family had a chance to survive."

Short Feather took his drum and closed his eyes.

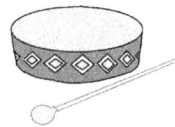

When Storm, Rain Catcher, and I returned to Dodge City, Maggie showed me a letter she had received from a friend in New Jersey. The letter was in response to Maggie's inquiry about an actor named Clive Cornelius. The friend was a supporter of the arts and knew many people who were active in the theater. She said that there was an itinerant actor and singer who had made the rounds of the East Coast. He called himself Clive Cornel, and his shows always did well because he was a very good singer and he had an exotic young girl who could sing so well people would go back two or three nights in a row just to hear her.

The letter said the troupe had been in New Jersey about two years ago and that they had headed south. Maggie's friend had heard that their goal was to play in New Orleans.

"I must go to New Orleans," I told Maggie.

Maggie said, "Short Feather, that was over two years ago. They could be anywhere now."

"I have to try. It is killing me not knowing where she is," I cried out.

"You need my help. I'll go with you," said Maggie.

And so we prepared to go to New Orleans, but it was not to be. I became a wanted man.

18

> "It is always good to help someone in need or in danger, but sometimes trouble is not far behind."
>
> —Short Feather

The year now is 1873. I am seventeen years old, and in town among whites, I maintained my big stupid Indian act. Actually, I was quite good at it as it became second nature. Most of the people who lived in Dodge City were kind to me. The soldiers and cowboys either ignored me or shoved me out of the way. I must have said, "Ken good Injun," ten thousand times in that year.

One day, in mid-May, the train was late getting in. The conductor, who knew me and seemed to like me, said that some wealthy men from the East had insisted that the train stop so that they could shoot buffalo that had been, unfortunately, grazing near the tracks. I was manning our "Original Indian Artifacts" booth alone since it was already after dark. Business was good that night. I sold almost everything I had brought to display.

On the way home after closing, I was walking through Dodge City. The moon was full and very bright. I did not need my lantern. Coming the other way was a pretty young woman who had always treated me well. Her name was Molly, and when we passed, she smiled and said, "Good evening, Ken. Did you have a nice day?"

"Yes-um, Ken good Injun," I said, looking down.

"I know you are, Ken, good night." She walked down the street.

I only walked a few paces when I heard a muffled scream, and turned around to see Molly being dragged into an alley by two men. One of the men had his hand over her mouth. There were two soldiers across the street. They saw what was going on but did nothing.

I ran into the alley. One of the men was the second stable private whom I had worked with at Fort Dodge. The other was also a soldier whom I had seen at the fort, but neither was wearing a uniform. Each had a six-shooter stuck in his belt.

"Now, Ken, you just run along. This ain't none o' yur business," said the stable private.

I call him "stable private" because I have refused, since that night, to ever say his name.

Standing as tall as I could, I said, "Ken say let friend Molly go."

The second man said, "Not a chance, moron. Now get lost."

I was about five paces away and did not move.

The second man let go of Molly and started to walk toward me as he reached for his gun. Storm taught me that, when in battle, to always react first and think about it later. Otherwise I would die young. Before the man could draw his gun or take two steps, my knife was buried in his chest up to the hilt.

The stable private let go of Molly and ran out of the alley. The two soldiers across the street had seen everything. I retrieved my knife and took Molly to the sheriff's office. There was no one there. Molly asked me to walk her home and said that she would talk to the sheriff in the morning. She lived in the big house at the end of the street, the house with the red light.

When I got home, I told Maggie, Snow, and Storm what had happened. They all said that I must leave immediately and not come back until they sent for me. Storm was the only one who knew where I was going. We settled on a Cheyenne/Arapaho village near Camp Supply in Oklahoma. There was a family there whom we had befriended on one of our trips.

Maggie gave me more money than I needed, and Storm loaded a packhorse with gifts and supplies for the family I was going to stay with. Everything I needed personally was already packed because Maggie and I were going to leave for New Orleans the next day.

Riding all night put a great distance between me and Dodge City. I stopped in a secluded gully that had a small creek running through it. Storm and I had stopped there before. This was in the late morning. I needed to rest my horses and get some sleep.

I pushed the horses and myself as fast and as far as we could go. I arrived at the village on the third day. Our friends took me in and were grateful for the gifts and supplies. They looked like they were starving and had lost two of their four children to disease since the last time I had been there. The food that was promised by the US government was so bad no one wanted to eat it, and those who did became ill. Weapons were not allowed. This left the Indians easy prey for rustlers and thieves. I was sickened by the plight of these poor, wretched human beings.

A month later, Storm arrived. It had taken him two weeks to get to the reservation because he was followed by some Long Knives and a Crow scout. It took many days to lose them.

He told me what had happened after I left. "The next morning, an officer from Fort Dodge, four troopers, and the sheriff showed up at Maggie's house. She met them outside. Snow and I listened from inside the house."

The sheriff spoke first. "Maggie, we're here for Ken. Where is he?"

"He is not here," said Maggie. "Why do you want him?"

"He killed one of my men, and would have killed another if he could have," said the army officer.

Maggie calmly said, "You know it was self-defense. Have you not talked to the woman that your men attacked and your two soldiers, who saw everything?"

The officer became angry and began to yell. "There was no woman, and none of my soldiers were in town except the two that stupid Indian attacked, and that's the truth. Now where is he, lady? You are obstructing justice."

"I don't think you know the meaning of the words *truth* or *justice*," said Maggie.

"Maggie," said the sheriff, "you need to tell us. Ken has been charged with murder. This is serious."

"I have no idea where he is. He ran away last night because he was afraid you would do exactly what you are doing," said Maggie, as she turned and walked back into the house.

"We need to search your house!" yelled the officer.

Maggie turned back to face them. "I know my rights. You can search my house when you have a warrant."

"Maggie, you know the judge won't be back till next month," said a frustrated sheriff.

Maggie smiled, turned, and walked into her house.

"Yeah, I guess you do know," mumbled the sheriff.

Storm told me that Maggie and Snow had gone to talk to Molly. They said she was really scared, and told them the army officer had threatened her and told her to keep her mouth shut. Maggie also talked to Private Jim Cable. He told her the two soldiers who knew the truth had been transferred to a unit in Texas that was fighting the Comanche. They were ordered to leave early in the morning after the incident.

Storm said to me, "Short Feather, I do not believe that you will be able to return to Dodge City. You stand out too much, and the people there are angry that an Indian killed a white man in their town. I don't understand this because the men around there seem to want to kill each other all the time."

Short Feather stopped drumming and opened his eyes. "Perhaps that is enough for this evening."

Breeze was sound asleep in Juanita's arms. Allison gently took her and put her in her crib in the nursery.

"I could hold her forever," said Juanita. "But, Grandfather, you cannot stop now. We want to know what happened next. It is all so sad that you could not return to your family."

"Yes, please go on. I could listen to you all night," said Jacob.

Short Feather chuckled. "You might be able to listen all night, but I most assuredly could not talk all night. I think I will stretch my legs. Juanita, will you pour me some coffee? And I wonder if there is any more of that crème brûlée."

Juanita got up and went to the kitchen. Short Feather was a little slower. He watched her walk away and said, "She is so beautiful, and such an amazing person. If I was ninety years younger…" He just let the statement hang, and gave Lee a grandfatherly look.

There was no more crème brûlée, but Allison helped Juanita find some chocolate chip cookies.

Short Feather spoke between sips of coffee and four cookies. "I was devastated. The thought that I would not be able to be with Sunrise and Maggie and the others was just too much for me. My hate began to grow even more."

When Short Feather was finished with his snack, he picked up his drum, closed his eyes, and continued.

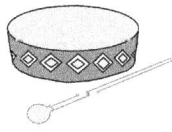

Storm had brought more supplies like flour, sugar, dried beef, beans, and even coffee. The family we were with was grateful. Storm stayed for three days and then said he needed to get back to Dodge City. I told him I would head to the mountains of Colorado, where my family had spent two winters before Washita.

The day after Storm left, a Cheyenne brave came to the lodge where I was staying. He was not well-liked in the village because he was known to be a spy for the Indian agent at Camp Supply. He had a letter that had obviously been opened. It was addressed to me from Maggie and was written in her version of written Cheyenne.

The spy took me outside and spoke quietly. "I was instructed not to tell you this. There are four Long Knives who will be here to get you in about two hours. They have been ordered to take you back to Fort Dodge, but if you go with them, you will no longer reside in this world. They will kill you."

I gave him a gold coin. It was clear that he was a spy for both sides. Leaving the rest of the money and the packhorse with my reservation family, I loaded up quickly and rode northwest. Reading the letter had to wait until I stopped to rest my horse.

When I was able to read the letter, I was very surprised and happy. Maggie said that Molly had talked to the sheriff and told him everything. Also, the two soldiers who had witnessed the attack reported the incident to their new commanding officer in Texas, who wrote a letter to the sheriff. The sheriff confronted the officer from Fort Dodge, who withdrew his charge against me, and the stable private was arrested for assault.

I went home.

19

> "Many people spend their lives searching for something that cannot be found. Wisdom knows when to stop."
>
> —Short Feather

I spent the next year and a half looking for Peppermint. I did go to New Orleans; Maggie could not go. Many people remembered the Clive Cornel Traveling Theater. All they could talk about was the exotic little girl with the amazing singing voice.

One local theater owner said, "They basically put me out of business for three nights. Everyone wanted to hear the girl. I think I remember that they called her Pepper. She could sing anything and melt the heart of every man in the room. I know, because I went to hear her twice. The women all wanted her for their daughter. I was sure glad they were a traveling show."

"Please, sir, when was that, and do you know where they went?" I asked as politely as I could.

The man thought for a moment. "Let's see, had to be late last year. They did some Christmas songs. I say 'they' because there was Clive, his two daughters, and the girl. Seems to me I heard they were headed west, maybe San Francisco."

The West. It was so big it boggled my mind. I did go to San Francisco, but no one there had ever heard of Clive Cornel or a troupe of one man, two women, and a fifteen- or sixteen-year-old girl. I went to every big city and talked to hundreds of people, but

Peppermint seemed to have disappeared from the face of the earth, along with Clive Cornel.

I managed to control my anger, frustration, and burning hate for the white man in general. Most treated me like a curiosity, never knowing how dangerous I really was. Because of my size, I could pass for much older than my teenage years, and my stupid act totally disarmed people.

In March of 1875, I gave up and went home. It was good to be home with my family. Sunrise was turning into a beautiful little girl, and Rain Catcher was becoming a second Thunderstorm.

Speaking of Storm, he was doing quite well with his business partner, the well-dressed man from the East who had bought all the artifacts in '73. Storm had even gone to the East and was a popular speaker, especially with churches. He was now a believer in Jesus, as were Sage Woman and Snow. He would tell his story and talk about the Indians and how they had been treated so poorly. He always had his original Indian artifacts to sell. The most popular items were the moccasins. The churches always took an offering to help the reservation Indians. Storm made sure every penny of that money went where it was intended.

Maggie's and Snow's store just kept growing. It did not take long before they discovered that the first thing cowboys wanted after long, hard cattle drives was not a bottle of whiskey and a woman but a bath and new clothes. Maggie had a bathhouse built behind the store and made sure there were always new duds on the shelves, especially hats and boots.

I figured I was home to stay even though the hate still burned within me. I could not accept that my people were condemned to being a defeated, abused, and used people.

Maggie, Storm, and Snow kept telling me, "God has a plan, and loves you. What happens in this life is unimportant compared to spending eternity with Him through Jesus Christ."

The hardest things for me to understand were how can a God of love allow such evil to exist, and why was it that some of the most vicious and evil men professed to follow Jesus? Men like Colonel Chivington of Sand Creek who was a Methodist minister. Why was it that soldiers would go to church on Sundays and then come to a peaceful Cheyenne village and murder my mother and father, taking my sister as a toy to play with? None of these things made sense to me.

Storm and I continued to take trips to Cheyenne and Arapaho villages on and off the reservations. We would trade for handmade items that Storm knew would sell. At one village in southern Colorado, we came across the family whom I had stayed with on the reservation near Camp Supply. They had finally had enough and decided to leave. This was a dangerous thing to do, but they determined it was more dangerous to stay. They were dying on the reservation.

The village was getting ready to move. They were on their way to a place in the far north where a medicine chief named Sitting Bull was gathering our people together to free our land of white tyranny. The more I heard of this, the more curious and interested I became. We were told that human beings from many tribes were leaving the reservations all over the west to join him.

20

"A good sense of humor never hurts."

—Short Feather

In June of 1875, I left my family to find Sitting Bull and see if the stories were true. Also, I had heard that some of the Washita captives were with Sitting Bull although I never did find any. Rushing Water, my favorite horse, was the only one I took. He was very big, very strong, had more endurance than I did, and at nineteen, I was in very good shape. We traveled well together, and I really enjoyed being out in the open and on my own with a goal that thrilled my heart. I did not know that one lone white man was following me.

We had been out for about a week and had a good night's rest. Rushing Water was ready to go at dawn, but he had to wait until I was ready. I decided to wear my Cheyenne clothes because they were much more comfortable, but I kept my white-man clothes rolled up and tied to Rushing Water. When I was ready, we headed for the open prairie. It was a beautiful day. We had not gone far when I felt Rushing Water falter and slump beneath me. In the same instant, I heard a gunshot.

Instinctively grabbing my rifle, I rolled off my horse and into some brush. There was another gunshot as I heard and felt a bullet go by, near to my head. I could tell that the shooter was close and directly in front of me in some rocks. There was a hole in Rushing Water's chest. He had already stopped breathing.

Finding that I was in a slight depression, I aimed my rifle toward the rocks, looking for the shooter. I saw a rifle come up and then a hat with a head in it. I aimed, took a deep breath, and let it out slowly as I gently squeezed the trigger. The head and hat dropped down below the rock, and I waited. The rifle stayed where it was, on the rock.

The world was quiet, so I decided to do a zigzag run toward the rocks, always watching the shooter's rifle, which stayed where it was. With a war cry, I ran around the rocks and found the stable private who had attacked Molly, with a bullet hole in his forehead. My war cry had scared away his horse. I never did find it.

I walked north for almost a month after my horse was shot out from under me. During that time, I saw no buffalo at all. It was hard to believe they had been wiped out so quickly and so completely. There had to be some somewhere—at least I prayed there were. I did find a small mule that appeared to be as happy to see me as I was to see him. He was too small for me to ride, but he seemed happy to carry my belongings. I called him Left Alone, and we became best of friends.

One day, Left Alone and I had been walking since early morning, and it was midafternoon when I saw smoke just beyond a hill in front of us. There was a creek on the east side of the hill, so we headed in that direction. I filled my water bags at the creek, and Left Alone took a long drink and started munching on the grass. Leaving him to eat, I headed toward the smoke.

It was a bright sunny afternoon, but it looked like storm clouds were forming in the west. As I came closer to the smoke, I began to crawl and was careful not to make noise. By the time I reached the edge of a gully, I could see lightning in the storm clouds, but I did not hear thunder for quite a while, and even then, it was muted. Below me was a campfire with the bodies of five white men scattered around it. They had been stripped to their underwear, but near one of them I saw a soldier's hat. All of them had had some hair taken from their heads. As I got closer, one of them moved.

I stood over him. It looked like he was shot in the shoulder, but there was blood everywhere, probably from the spot where he lost some hair.

"Why can't you damn Indians just go away and let me die?" said the man. But he did not seem to be talking to me, more to himself.

"Is that what you want to do?" I asked.

"Well I'll be, it speaks English. You are possibly the biggest Indian I've ever seen. Are you going to kill me?"

"No," I said, as I picked him up to carry him back to where Left Alone was. I laid him by the creek and washed his wounds. A bullet had gone clean through his shoulder and amazingly had not hit bone or anything important. There was a gash on his leg, which I cleaned and wrapped. His head was another matter. It was clear he was going to have a bald spot.

"Why are you doing this?" the man asked.

"You are no danger to me, and I don't kill helpless animals except for food, and you don't look very tasty."

"Ain't life a hoot? I'm almost killed by Indians, and then I'm rescued by a giant Indian with a sense of humor, who speaks better English than me."

"Besides all of that, I am sure you would do the same for me," I said, looking into his eyes.

He looked away and said, "I ain't so sure." Then he passed out. He had lost a lot of blood.

After unloading Left Alone, I set up camp and made some elk stew. I did not have much dried meat, so it was more like soup. The man now seemed to be sleeping, but after a while, I woke him up with a damp cloth. He gratefully ate the soup, laid back, and was again sound asleep.

In the morning, I woke up to him asking, "What's your name?"

"Short Feather, and my mule is Left Alone."

"Weird name, and not too many people name a mule. My name is Jim Worthington—Sgt. Jim Worthington. Are you Cheyenne?"

"Yes," I said.

"Thought so, but all you Indians sure do look alike."

"Yes," I said. "I feel the same way about you whites."

Just then Left Alone picked up his head from the grass, and his ears went straight forward. Before I could grab my rifle, we were surrounded by five Cheyenne braves with five rifles pointed at us—two at the soldier and three at me.

"What are you doing with this white man?" asked one of the braves in Cheyenne.

"I have always believed it is good to keep at least one alive to tell other whites how savage we are. Maybe they will become frightened and leave our land."

"I think he is making fun of us," said another one of the braves. "We should kill both of them."

"What are they saying?" asked the sergeant.

"They think they should kill both of us," I said, as I heard horses coming.

"Well, it sure has been nice knowing you, Short Feather," said the sergeant with a wink and a smile.

Ten more braves rode up to my campsite in a cloud of dust. They had with them about fifteen more Indian ponies and six Long Knife horses. Five of the braves were wearing Long Knife shirts, which had obviously been taken from the sergeant and the dead soldiers. The shirts had the insignia of the Seventh Cavalry.

When the dust cleared, the leader of the band dismounted and signaled the five braves to lower their weapons. He was a small man but walked like a man who was in charge and knew it. It was clear to me he was a Dog Soldier and a leader of Dog Soldiers. He also looked familiar.

Walking up to me, smiling, he said, "Short Feather, how is your nose?"

"My nose is just fine now, thank you, although it took quite a few days for the swelling to go down. Does yours still bleed easily, Little Hawk?" I asked.

Little Hawk laughed, and we embraced, patting each other on the back. He introduced me to his men. "This human being is Short Feather. He is one of the bravest and best Dog Soldiers I have ever known. He killed my brother, and no one is to touch a hair on his head, except me."

His men looked confused but obviously respected him. They had heard the story of the Duel in the Grass, and looking at me and then at Little Hawk, it was clear they were amazed he had bested me.

Four braves were sent out by Little Hawk to stand guard. The rest watered the horses and settled down to rest. They had food, which they shared with me and the sergeant. He had no idea what was going on or what was said because all of our talk was in Cheyenne. Two fierce-looking braves sat down to eat, with the sergeant between them.

"Why have you kept this white man alive?" asked Little Hawk.

"I will tell you what I told him when he asked the same question. I do not kill helpless animals for no reason. Besides, I did not think he would survive. Also, if he lived, I thought it would be a good idea for him to tell his fellow soldiers that we are fierce fighters and that we are fighting to protect our land and families and way of life."

Little Hawk scratched his head. "Do you really think that will help, Short Feather?"

I thought for a moment. "If it makes some of them hesitate in battle, even just a little, it can give us an edge."

"Do you know why we attacked and killed these Long Knives?" asked Little Hawk.

"No, I do not," I answered.

"Two of my men, Light Horse and Gray Bull, were tracking and watching them. One of the Long Knives saw a group of twelve Arapaho traveling across a meadow. He shot into the group and killed a woman. She was with child. Her husband, who was young and inexperienced, charged toward the soldiers. They killed him too before they ran away. My men were too far away to help. Gray Bull stayed with the travelers, and Light Horse returned to tell me what had happened."

I became angry and looked at the sergeant. He saw my look, and seemed to shrink down and become more nervous than he already was. I spoke to him, "I have been told that you shot an innocent woman and then killed her husband. What do you have to say?"

The sergeant looked at the ground. "It was one of my men, Private Peterson. A man I did not like because killing to him was fun. My unit was detailed to hunt game, and when we saw the Indians, I told my men to just ignore them. Peterson aimed at the Indians and fired. He was laughing. I tried to stop him—really, I did—and then one of the Indians charged toward us yelling and screaming. He only had a bow and a knife. Peterson shot him too. We ran because Indians on horseback were riding toward us from the hills to our right."

"Did you know that the woman was pregnant?" I asked.

"Oh, dear Lord, no, I did not," the sergeant cried out.

I told Little Hawk what the sergeant had said. He confirmed that only one soldier had fired.

"Grandfather," interrupted Juanita. "I don't understand how you can remember all of these details and names from so long ago."

Short Feather opened his eyes and stopped drumming. "I wonder at this also, little one. It is both a blessing and a curse. But I think it is time to stop. I do not know how much longer my voice will last."

"Yes, of course," said Lee. "We are asking too much of you."

"Oh no, this has been a wonderful day that I have been able to spend with this beautiful family," Short Feather objected. "My two favorite young people joined us for a fantastic dinner, and I got to tell more of my story to people who actually care. A memory I will cherish forever is that I got to take a nap with a four-month-old baby sleeping on my chest. The perfect vision of Juanita is now burned into my mind, along with my mother, Peppermint, and my wife. I am grateful to the Great Spirit that he has given me this day."

Lee answered, "It has been a special day for all of us. Tomorrow is Sunday. Maybe we should let you rest."

"I would really like to continue. I don't know why, but I feel a sense of urgency," said Short Feather with a smile. "Maybe it is because I am one hundred and ten years old. Normal people don't live that long."

"Now you are trying to tell us you are normal," quipped Juanita.

Everyone laughed.

Short Feather thought for a moment. "I do have my Bible study with Charley in the morning. I would be free after ten."

"Juanita and I would like to come to your Bible study again," said Lee. "We would just be quiet and listen."

"Speak for yourself, White Tears. I make no such promises," said Juanita.

There was more laughter.

"It would be a pleasure to have both of you come," said Short Feather. "Charley and I welcome all input, even from a sassy little senorita."

"I have a great idea," said Jacob. "We will be home from church by eleven. You could come back here then, and we could sit on the patio. It is supposed to be a beautiful day."

"Yes, I could make a light lunch with Juanita's help," said Allison. "You could bring Charley. Who is Charley?"

"Charley is a good friend and brother in the Lord," said Short Feather. "I think he would love to come, thank you."

Lee took Short Feather home first, then Juanita. They sat in his car and talked until almost midnight, parked in front of Juanita's home. Jose finally came out and said it was time for Juanita to come in.

21

> "The men that make the decisions and give the orders seldom see the suffering."
>
> —Sergeant Worthington

At 9:00 a.m. the next day, Lee knocked at the Trujio door.

Jose answered the door. "Come in and sit for a minute. Juanita is not ready yet."

"What were you and Juanita talking about for so long last night?" asked Jose.

Lee spoke quietly, "Joe, we talked about everything: politics, religion, education, and our dreams for the future. Juanita did most of the talking. I enjoyed listening to her. She is very smart. Oh, and just before you came out to get her, I told her that I love her."

"And what did she say?" asked Jose.

"That is none of your business, my brother," said Juanita.

She was standing behind them in a yellow sundress that came just to her knees. Her hair was loose, falling over her shoulders, with the buffalo tail attached perfectly on the right side.

Lee caught his breath and stood up.

Jose laughed. "I may not let you see my sister again. Not for her protection, but yours. Every time she walks into the room, you stop breathing."

Juanita took Lee's arm, and they left to go to Short Feather's.

The Bible study was lively as they continued in the book of Matthew. Charley said that he had no plans for the rest of the day and he would love to meet Dr. and Mrs. Bronson.

When they arrived at the Bronson home, Jacob welcomed them with a big smile, and Allison began taking pictures. Breeze was in her high chair, happily eating Cheerios. Charley was a little surprised to see that the Bronsons were black like him. No one had told him. No one had thought about it.

Allison suggested they sit on the patio. She brought out some chips and cookies and a new snack called Bugles. Short Feather especially liked the Bugles. It was again a beautiful day.

Short Feather took his drum and began drumming softly. Closing his eyes, he began speaking.

We stayed at the campsite for three more days. Little Hawk sent his men out three or four at a time to scout the area and watch for Long Knives. Gray Bull returned on the third day and said that the Arapaho travelers had reached the Cheyenne village safely.

Sgt. Jim Worthington was recovering from his wounds and gaining strength. We had many conversations during the three days. At one point, he said he had been at Washita with Custer. My hand automatically went to my six-shooter, and his hands went up. This caused him some pain because of his shoulder.

"Whoa, Short Feather, I did not take part in the killing. I was ordered to round up the ponies," said the sergeant. "Were you there?"

"I was there," I said through clenched teeth. "Both of my parents were killed, and my sister was taken away."

This was the first time in many years I had thought about the way my parents had died. I had buried the memories, but now they were flooding my mind and consuming me. I came close to killing the sergeant then and there. It was hard for me to let go of my pistol.

I could see the sergeant was sincere when he said, "I am very sorry for your loss. I can only imagine the pain you must feel."

"Why? Why?" I exclaimed, choking up. "I don't understand why you white men feel that you must kill all of us Indians. I understand war. My people have been at war with the Crow and other tribes for many years, but there has always been honor among us. Women and children and the old ones were never slaughtered like you white men have done. And why kill the ponies? I can still hear their cries from Washita."

"It is called strategy," said the sergeant slowly and quietly. "We had a bad war among ourselves, North and South, and the North won by destroying the South's ability to fight. Strategy is why the ponies and buffalo have been destroyed. If you cannot feed and clothe and shelter yourselves, then you cannot fight. It is sad that strategy does not take into account suffering. This is another example of the end justifies the means—winning becomes more important than how you win."

"Do you hold to this kind of thinking?" I asked.

The sergeant was quiet for a few moments, and then said, "No, I do not, but I am a soldier, and my duty is to follow orders. The men that make the decisions and give the orders seldom see the suffering."

The next day, Little Hawk gave me an Indian pony, the largest and strongest of his herd. He gave the sergeant one of the Long Knife horses. Left Alone would be taken to the Cheyenne village and cared for until I arrived. My plan was to take the sergeant as close as I could to his unit, turn him loose, and then join the village. Little Hawk assigned two of his braves to go with us, Dark Cloud and Talon. Both were brave and fierce fighters who revered Little Hawk.

Before we left, Little Hawk spoke to Sergeant Worthington. I translated, of course. "You have been fortunate that Short Feather is the one that found you alive. If I ever see you again, I will kill you."

We had traveled two days when we spotted a Long Knife patrol, and I released the sergeant. I told him to tell his people what I had told him and to remember what Little Hawk had said.

As he left, he said, "Thank you, Short Feather, I consider you a friend."

I said nothing more.

The Cheyenne village was nestled in a valley with a good stream of crystal clear water. The village was not large but was growing every day with people arriving from the south and from reservations to the east. There was a spirit of hope and excitement that I wanted but could never acquire.

Little Hawk was very good to me. He found a lodge for me, and I ate almost every meal with his family. His wife, Blue Sky, was beautiful, smart, devoted to her husband, and a very good cook. They had two small children, a boy and a girl, named Sky Hawk and River. Little Hawk's family was a joy, and they treated me like I was one of them.

Blue Sky had a younger sister who visited often. Her name was Willow, and I fell in love with her the first time I saw her. This was new to me, and I became a shy bumbling idiot, this time for real. When Willow was visiting, I tended to spill things and run into things and my speech became tangled and ridiculous. Many times I found that I could not breathe when she entered the tepee.

Soon it became clear that Willow felt the same way about me, although I could never figure out why. She was beautiful and small and seemed so fragile, with eyes that always sparkled and a smile that could melt a glacier. Her hair and clothes were always perfect. She was perfect, but she did not live very long.

Short Feather spoke these words slowly, the last sentence even slower. The drumming stopped, and he became very quiet, a tear running down his cheek. Lee and Juanita were holding hands, and Juanita put her head on Lee's shoulder. Jacob and Allison were also holding hands, and Allison was crying softly. Charley had his eyes closed, and they all sat quietly for a number of minutes.

Breeze was sitting in her high chair and decided that enough was enough. She let out a high-pitched yell that opened everyone's eyes and definitely got their attention. They all laughed, which made Breeze laugh and wave her arms.

"Perhaps this is a good time to stop for lunch," said Allison. "Juanita and I will make some sandwiches and feed Breeze."

In the kitchen, Allison said to Juanita, "It is apparent to me that you and Lee are becoming quite close, but I sense some hesitation on your part."

"He told me that he loves me," said Juanita.

Allison smiled and took Juanita's hand. "That fact is very clear by the way he looks at you and the way he treats you. So what is the problem? Do you not love him?"

Juanita began to cry softly. "I have had three other good men tell me that they loved me. Each of them proposed marriage, and I turned them down. My feelings for Lee are different, and I find it hard to put them into words, even for myself. I care for him very much and feel alone and lost when I am not with him."

"Sounds like love to me," said Allison. "So I will ask again, what is the problem?"

"The problems are many," said Juanita, as she went back to making sandwiches. "First, I am Mexican and he is white. Jose says this is not a problem, but Lee and I are from two totally different cultures. My family is Catholic and he is Presbyterian. We have only known each other for a short time, and we are different in so many ways."

"Except for one," said Allison quietly. "You love each other."

"Yes," said Juanita with frustration. "I do love him very much. Fortunately, he has not asked me to marry him. Maybe he won't and the problems won't matter."

Jacob came to help take the sandwiches to the patio. While they were eating, Allison asked, "What were you men talking about while we were gone?"

"Oh, politics, the condition of the world, religion," said Charley.

"And women," said Lee.

Short Feather laughed. "I don't think you were supposed to tell them that, White Tears. These sandwiches are wonderful, Warm Breeze, and what were you and Buffalo Tail talking about?"

Juanita looked at Allison.

"I cannot take credit for the sandwiches," Allison said. "Juanita made them, and yes, they are wonderful. And, Short Feather, I have not heard you refer to Charley with an Indian name." She was trying to change the subject.

"I have known Charley for ten years, and he is my teacher and good friend," said Short Feather. "I named him Man of the Great Spirit. That is a long name, so I just call him Charley, which, to me, means the same thing."

Allison asked, "Charley, when did you come to know our Lord?"

"That is a long and difficult story," said Charley. "But I will try to summarize.

"As a teenager, I was not a good person. We lived in Alabama, and my mama was a cook for a rich white family. They were demanding and did not treat her well, but it was no different for other black folk anywhere in Alabama. I never knew my father. He died before I was two years old. Mama said he died in a sawmill accident, but I found out when I was sixteen that he had been lynched because a white woman said he looked at her wrong. I was a bitter and angry young man and caused a lot of trouble. God did not figure into my life at all. I was an atheist.

"One day, my uncle sat me down and said that I should run away and join the navy, that I was not wanted or welcome there any longer. So at eighteen, I joined the navy. The navy gave me two choices: I could work on the docks loading ships, or I could be a steward on a ship. I figured that on a ship I might get to see some of the world, so I opted for the ship.

"I had my share of trouble over the next twenty-three years, but the navy did turn me into a better person. I learned to accept my station in life and hide my anger. I still did not believe in God. Then it was 1941, and the Japanese bombed Pearl Harbor. I was the captain's steward on a minesweeper headed for Hawaii when we got the news.

"My captain had a habit of praying and reading his Bible every day. I asked him about it and told him I was an atheist. He looked sad and asked me what I believed would happen when I died. I said I did not know but suspected that there would just be nothing. I would simply cease to exist. Then he asked me a question that caused me to do a lot of thinking. He asked, 'What if you're wrong?'

"Over the next few months, we talked as often as we could. The captain gave me a Bible and told me about Jesus. When we were alone in his cabin, he treated me like an equal and a friend. I had never experienced this kind of treatment from a white man, and what was even more extraordinary was that he was my commanding officer. It did not take long for me to overcome my sinful pride and accept God's gift of salvation."

"What a wonderful testimony," said Allison.

22

"Love is a choice and we must choose it."

—Willow

The lunch dishes were cleared, and little Breeze was put down for a nap. Allison and Juanita brought out iced tea and soft drinks.

When everyone was settled, Juanita spoke to Short Feather, "Grandfather, will you be able to tell us about Willow and what happened to her?"

"Yes, I will, but I must not get ahead of myself," responded Short Feather. "Please be patient with me. I want to tell you everything, but some parts are difficult."

With drum in hand and eyes closed, Short Feather continued.

Willow and I were together during the daytime whenever I was in the village. Much of the time, however, I was out with Little Hawk and his men on patrol or hunting. The village was growing too big for the valley we were in, so the leaders decided to move. Little Hawk was tasked with finding a new site with good grass for the ponies and a more abundant supply of water.

In the village, Willow was a delight to be with. We took many long walks together and talked for hours. Willow liked to talk about family and friends and the love they had for each other and all human beings, even the bad ones. She even said once that we should love the white man. This was hard for me to understand.

I told her about Maggie and Storm and the rest of my adopted family and that I loved them, but how can I love those who killed my parents, stole my sister, and wanted to destroy us? She said that only the Great Spirit could help me to understand and that I should pray about it. I did pray and asked for help to understand the kind of love that Willow was talking about. The Great Spirit answered my prayers many months later, but in a hard and difficult way.

In late August of 1875, I went to Little Hawk and Blue Sky and told them I wished to marry Willow. They were very pleased, and Blue Sky, Willow's sister, offered to talk to her mother and grandmother. I had no other family to speak for me.

One big problem was that I did not have any ponies to give to Willow's family. Little Hawk offered to give me two ponies because I had been such a good friend and had freed his brother from his misery by providing him with an honorable death. This was unacceptable to me because I wanted to earn the ponies and show how committed I was to Willow. I therefore offered to hunt for and bring to Little Hawk and his family six elk or deer in the next two weeks. This was not an easy thing to do, but in two weeks, with little sleep or rest, I delivered four deer and two elk to Little Hawk. He, in turn, gave one of each to Willow's family.

In the meantime, Blue Sky had talked to Willow's mother and grandmother on three separate occasions. This was necessary because I was not well-known in the village, and the women needed to be sure that I would be a good husband for Willow. They already knew I was a good warrior because I was a Dog Soldier, and the proofs of my hunting skills were now drying in the sun. Willow's family gave their approval and submitted the proposal to the village elders. After the elders approved, Blue Sky reported that I had permission to pursue Willow.

Willow's father was a great warrior and well respected by all in the village. His name was Son of the Wind, and when he summoned me, I was quite nervous. Little Hawk laughed and said I should be. His father-in-law—and mine to be—was very intimidating. When I entered his lodge, he was sitting, and looked at me for a long time. Finally, he motioned for me to sit.

"I will tell you what I told Little Hawk," began Son of the Wind. "My daughters are more important to me than my own life." He paused and looked into my eyes. "Or yours."

A few days later, Little Hawk provided two beautiful ponies, which I tied in front of Willow's lodge. I stayed a respectable distance away and watched. After about two hours, Willow's mother came out, moved the ponies to the back of the tepee, and left. This act gave me permission to lie down in front of the door to Willow's home.

Soon, Willow came out and held open the flap for me to enter, and then she left. At this point, I was married, but Willow did not come in until late in the afternoon when she entered to prepare our evening meal. We were now husband and wife.

I said before that Willow was small and beautiful. That was true, but I also said she seemed so fragile. On that I could not have been more wrong. I discovered very quickly that she was strong and tough. We did everything together, from carrying water and firewood to hunting and butchering our kill. As was the custom, she always walked behind me but never had a problem keeping up, and sometimes, she appeared to be pushing me to go faster. Willow also turned out to be a very good shot with a rifle, after I taught her what Thunderstorm had taught me.

Juanita interrupted, "Grandfather, you say that it was your custom for your wife to walk behind you. Was this to show that she was inferior or subservient?"

Short Feather stopped the drum and opened his eyes. "Certainly not, my little Buffalo Tail. It was the husband's responsibility to lead the way and clear the trail of any danger to his wife. Also, most trails were narrow, and it was impracticable to walk side by side. Even on horseback, the man led the way to protect his wife."

"Thank you, Grandfather," said Juanita.

Short Feather took a long drink of water, closed his eyes, and continued drumming.

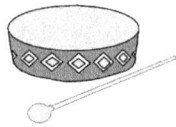

In what must have been October of 1875, Willow told me that she was with child. I could not have been happier or more frightened. Our world was in turmoil, and to make matters worse, there were three midwives in our village, and it became a battle of wills as to which one would care for Willow. She was very popular. Thankfully, my mother-in-law made the decision and settled the issue. Willow's grandmother came to stay with us. This concerned me at first, but soon, I came to love and accept her as part of my family.

Except for some morning sickness, Willow never missed a beat. She would not let me or her grandmother pamper her, even though we tried. She insisted that she continue to do all that she had done before. She seemed to grow stronger and became more beautiful every day. I cannot think of a time that she was not smiling or laughing. That winter was cold and difficult, but Willow filled my life with so much love and warmth that I hardly noticed the cold except when I was away from her on patrol. That was very difficult.

In the early spring of 1876, our village moved north until we finally found Sitting Bull and his Hunkpapa people at Sundance Creek, a tributary of the Little Bighorn River. It was early June. A few days after we arrived there, my daughter Aspen was born. It took great effort on Grandmother's part to keep Willow down and quiet for even a few days. Soon, she was up and resuming her duties, plus taking care of the baby and helping other families who were arriving every day. Beside the Hunkpapa, there were human beings of the Oglala, Minneconjou, and Sans Arc tribes—all part of the Lakota Sioux people. Also there were some Arapaho mixed in with us Cheyenne. My guess would be that there were six thousand in all, with about twelve hundred warriors. The village was an amazing sight, but for me, the most amazing sight of all was my little daughter, Aspen.

Little Hawk and I were able to meet Sitting Bull. I was only with him for a few minutes, but it was long enough for me to understand why people followed him. He was very strong of character and projected much wisdom. I did have a sense of foreboding, because I could tell that he hated the whites as much as I did; maybe more. For some reason, this did not instill confidence in me, and I did not understand why.

Returning home to Willow made me feel much better. She loved everyone and would often say, "It is easy to love those who love you. The real test of one's character is when one can love those who are bad and do hateful things."

A number of days later, Sitting Bull sent word that the village was going to move a little farther north to a better location. It was on the Little Bighorn River, and would have more room for our large number of lodges. Even more people were known to be on their way to join us, and there was better grass for the ponies that numbered more than two thousand.

On the sixteenth of June, a brave named Little Hawk (not my friend Little Hawk) rode into the village and reported that he had seen a large number of Long Knives coming from the south. He said they had crossed the Tongue River and were heading our way.

A call from the young men went out to form up to confront and stop the enemy. Sitting Bull and most of the older men felt it would be better to wait and not travel over twenty miles to a battle. The young men prevailed, however, and we left the village that evening.

Willow wanted to come with me, but I insisted that she stay with Aspen even though she could shoot and fight as well as most men.

We were about one thousand strong, and were led by Crazy Horse. After riding most of the night, we rested the horses early in the morning. The braves did not rest but prepared for battle. The battle itself was confusing to me. I had never fought with that many braves against so many Long Knives. There were also a good number of the Crow tribes that joined the Long Knives against us, and they were the first fighters we encountered.

After driving the Crows back to the main lines of the enemy, the battle became a series of advances, retreats, and moves. There were many times that I never saw the enemy, and in the entire day, I only fired ten of the twenty bullets that I had. Most of our fighters did not have guns, but they all fought bravely with the weapons they had. In the end, we caused the Long Knives to stop their advance, an event that Crazy Horse considered a victory.

The Long Knives called the fight the Battle of the Rosebud because they were at the Rosebud River. We called it the Battle Where the Woman Saved Her Brother. This was because a woman actually did ride into the middle of an intense fight under much fire from the enemy and save her brother. Little Hawk and I were sad because two of his men had been killed in the battle. They were our friends.

On returning to the village, we found that it had been moved to the Little Bighorn near the fields that we called the Greasy Grass.

Willow had already set up our lodge and was helping others while Grandmother took care of Aspen, who was now smiling and laughing as much as her mother.

If anyone had told me that so many Indians of different tribes would join together in one place, I would have laughed in their face. Each group had its own chief and war chief, but all submitted to the leadership of Sitting Bull and Crazy Horse. It was an amazing thing to see. I was concerned, however, that even this place would not be able to support so many people and horses.

On June 25, 1876, Little Hawk was summoned to meet with one of the subchiefs who were with Crazy Horse. He asked me to go with him. When we got to the south end of the village, we heard gunfire.

Running out of the village, we saw a large group of braves fighting Long Knives who were coming up toward the village. I had my rifle and six-shooter, as did Little Hawk, and as we ran to join the fight, we saw that the white soldiers had been stopped and were heading for the trees by the river to our left. This appeared to be the only way they could escape. Little Hawk and I headed that way.

The soldiers stopped and began firing from the forest. Little Hawk and I crawled and used what cover we could. Soon, we were close to a group of five soldiers who did not know we were there. They were occupied by a large number of braves farther to our right. We fired, killing two, and then charged the remaining three, who turned to run away.

I was near one, so I drew my six-shooter and pulled the trigger. It did not fire. The soldier heard the click, stopped, and turned around with his pistol aimed at my head. I was shocked to see that it was Sgt. Jim Worthington, the soldier I had saved the previous year. He also looked shocked and, as he lowered his gun, said, "Short Feather?"

I heard a gun fire from my left, and the sergeant slumped to the ground with a hole in his chest.

Little Hawk stood over the dead sergeant and said, "You were right, Short Feather. Your kindness did make him hesitate."

Light Horse, one of Little Hawk's braves, rode toward us. He was leading our horses, and when he got to us, he said that more Long Knives were coming toward the north end of the village and that while they were still a ways off, we were needed. Our Cheyenne lodges were all at the north end. I had great fear for Willow and Aspen, as did Little Hawk for his family. We could see that the soldiers were falling back across the river and were contained by our braves. It was clear that we were not needed there, so we followed Light Horse north.

Short Feather stopped drumming and opened his eyes. His hands were shaking.

"Perhaps this would be a good time for a break," said Dr. Bronson. "I think you should lie down and rest. I would like to check your vitals, Grandfather. Your breathing seems to be labored."

"That sounds like a good idea, Healing Breeze," said Short Feather.

Dr. Bronson took Short Feather into the family room and had him lie on the couch. After about fifteen minutes, Dr. Bronson came back out.

All were concerned, and Juanita asked, "Is he okay, Dr. Bronson?"

Dr. Bronson sat down. "Yes, he is doing fine. For a person one hundred and ten years old, he has a very strong heart. Actually, I am quite surprised at how healthy he is. His blood pressure is a little high, but he is concerned about going on with his story. He really wants to tell all of it."

"Should I go in and sit with him?" asked Juanita.

"He asked to be left alone for fifteen or twenty minutes and then I should get him," said the doctor. "He also said that you want to study to be a nurse and that you would be starting your studies in the fall. I think that is wonderful, and if there is anything I can do to help, please let me know."

Juanita smiled. "Thank you so much, but what Grandfather probably did not tell you is that he has set up a trust fund to finance my education and to help Lee with his. We are very grateful."

"Praise God," said Charley.

"What an amazing man," Allison added.

Short Feather walked out to the patio. He looked refreshed even though he had rested for only a few minutes. "I hope you were not talking about me behind my back."

"Why would you think that, old man?" teased Juanita, as she got up and helped him to his chair.

"Please, little Buffalo Tail, sit by me," requested Short Feather.

Allison provided a large pillow and placed it in front of Short Feather by his right knee. Taking up his drum, Short Feather gave it to Juanita as she sat on the pillow. He smiled and nodded. Juanita began to tap the same gentle rhythm. Both closed their eyes. Short Feather softly stroked the buffalo tail in Juanita's hair and began to speak.

The events of the rest of that day are not all clear to me. Little Hawk and I arrived at the Cheyenne village and found that Son of the Wind, Willow's father, was leaving with a large number of braves to confront the enemy. Willow was on her horse and had her rifle. Her father was telling her that she must stay with the other women. I tried to tell her that her father was correct.

Willow yelled as she rode off, "I have a right to defend my home and family."

Her father and I followed. There were many braves ahead of us and even more behind. Most had bows and arrows. Those who had guns did not have many bullets, and all needed to be careful not to hit other Indians. There were so many that this was a great concern.

Son of the Wind and I passed Willow. Her horse was smaller and not trained for battle.

The Long Knives began firing at us, and many braves went down. I could see, however, that we greatly outnumbered the soldiers, and would soon have them surrounded.

As I raised my rifle to fire, I heard a cry from behind me. I turned and saw Willow's horse without her. She was in the grass facedown. Jumping from my horse, I ran to her and cradled her in my arms, but she was not breathing.

The next thing I remember is that we were back at the village and Little Hawk was telling me that Son of the Wind had died of his wounds. He never knew his daughter had been killed.

Our family suffered great loss that day, and the grief was overwhelming. There is no way I can describe the sorrow and hate that took me into a darkness from which I did not think I could recover.

Juanita stopped tapping the drum, and Short Feather opened his eyes. They both had tears. Short Feather continued to stroke the buffalo tail in Juanita's hair.

All the listeners had moist eyes, and Short Feather spoke to them. "I do not know why, but telling this to you has taken a heavy burden from my heart that has been there far too long. I have never been able to think of Willow without pain, but now my memories are soft and quiet and peaceful. I think I will see her again soon. I feel certain that she is with Jesus even though I don't think she ever heard His name."

"Praise God," said Charley. Everyone said, "Amen," except Juanita, who looked a little confused.

Charley said, "Juanita, you look troubled."

Juanita thought for a few moments. "I know that the Catholic Church has its rules and requirements to achieve salvation, and so do Protestants. But Willow was not exposed to either, and yet you all believe that Willow is with Jesus. I want to believe that too, but I don't understand."

Short Feather smiled. "May I respond to that, Charley?"

"Of course, and if I disagree, I will certainly speak up," said Charley.

"The Great Spirit, God, is not limited by our understanding or lack of it," said Short Feather. "Nor is He limited by our rules, regulations, or interpretations. He knows every person's heart and interacts with each of us individually regardless of our culture or the time in which we live. I would never presume to say what God can or cannot do. If God wants Willow to be with Him, and I cannot see why He would not, then she is. It is important to say, however, that if an individual hears the Gospel of Jesus Christ and rejects it, choosing not to believe, that person is responsible and judged accordingly."

"I don't think I could have put it better," said Charley.

"Oh my, Grandfather," said Allison. "You just cleared up a lot of my questions with that short statement."

Short Feather smiled. "I think I would like to go on with my story. It is still early in the afternoon."

"Just let me check on Breeze, I'll be right back," said Allison.

When Allison returned with a sleepy but awake baby, Short Feather closed his eyes, and Juanita tapped the drum.

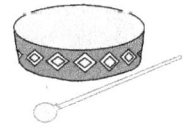

Sitting Bull and the rest of the chiefs realized that even though they had achieved a great victory, the large composite village was now vulnerable. Many Long Knives were known to be converging, and no location that we knew of could support such a large village. Wild game was our staple, and we needed grass for our animals. We did not have the luxury of wagons loaded with supplies, like our enemy, and they did not have their families to protect.

It was decided that the tribes needed to disperse. Some went back to the reservations, which Little Hawk and I rejected. Sitting Bull and many of his people went north and eventually into Canada.

Bright Star, my mother-in-law; Willow's grandmother; and my little daughter, Aspen, were now my family and responsibility. After we buried our dead, we traveled south with Little Hawk and his family. Three of Little Hawk's braves decided to come with us. This meant that we had five lodges and eighteen human beings. We felt that our small numbers would not draw attention. All of the men were skilled hunters and fighters.

In Colorado, we found a quiet valley with a good stream, and prepared for the winter. I was not a pleasant person to be around. Missing Willow terribly, I sank further into the darkness that hate causes. All I could think of was my hate for the Long Knives and the people who sent them to imprison us on reservations or kill us.

Killing all of them in the most terrible way dominated my thoughts. I was angry at everyone, including the Great Spirit. Bright Star and Grandmother grew impatient with me. I found myself isolated and alone. Even Little Hawk avoided me. I paid little attention to my baby daughter.

One evening, in the late fall, I was sitting in my lodge, staring at the fire. Grandmother brought Aspen and placed her in my arms.

"Your daughter needs you. Willow is very disappointed in you," was all she said as she left us alone.

Looking at my daughter, I began to cry. My heart was near to bursting with the pain and anguish that caused me to sob and scream; little Aspen began to cry. I got up and went out of my lodge. To my surprise, every member of our small village was standing there. I handed little Aspen to Grandmother.

"I will return a different human being, or I will not return," I said, as I walked toward the mountain taking nothing with me, not even my rifle or knife.

23

"God will speak to us, but we must learn to listen."

—Short Feather

I walked for most of the night. It was cold, but I did not notice. The moon was not at its brightest, but I was able to see where I was going most of the time. My thoughts were disorganized and confused. I did not want to be the despicable and vile person I was becoming.

As I walked, I looked up at the sky. The stars were bright and filled my vision. Something stopped me. It was almost like a hand on my chest, although I felt nothing. When I looked down, I saw that I was one step from the edge of a cliff with rocks about two hundred feet below. With that one step, I would have fallen to my death. The thought crossed my mind that maybe that was not a bad idea, but little Aspen's tiny face came to me.

Stopping where I was, I sat on the ground and looked up at the stars for a very long time. They began to fade as the sun was coming up. Thoughts were rushing through my mind, so I stood and put out my arms and yelled as loud as I could, "Great Spirit, Creator, and Father of this earth, I asked you to teach me how to love, and all you have done is taught me how to hate."

The world around me became totally quiet. The light from the sun began to reveal one of the most beautiful sights I had ever seen. It was, in fact, like I was seeing it for the first time. I looked out at mountains and valleys and trees, and far below me was a stream. In the distance, I saw five tepees with smoke coming from the cooking fires. Wonder filled my mind. Words began to come into my mind. I heard no voice, the world remained quiet.

These are the words that came to me: "If I can love you, you can love My children. Hate is natural to you. Love is a choice and takes effort. You are wondering, Who are My children? But you already know. When you can love the worst of them, you will understand My love. Start with the best and the easiest one to love: your daughter."

I stood for a long time pondering these words, which were written into my mind much like the words written in Maggie's book. The first thing I had to do was to admit I knew who the children of the Great Spirit were. I thought about Maggie, Sgt. Jim Worthington, and the other white people who had treated me well and shown themselves to be good and kind. For the first time in my life, I included all white people to be human beings and children of the Great Spirit.

I began to pray out loud with a strong voice. "Father, the earth and all it contains are your creation. Thank you for allowing me to be part of it. I belong to you. You know that I love my daughter. Please help me to love her more and to learn to love all of your children. I know that I am not capable of doing this on my own, but with your help, I will prevail. From this day on and for the rest of my life, I will live each day with love in my heart. This is my promise to you."

It had been many hours since I had slept, and I was very tired. I decided to rest before I went back to my family. Lying down on the ground, I went instantly into a deep sleep. When I awoke, the sun was almost directly overhead, and an animal was licking my hand.

To my shock, I saw that it was a mountain lion almost as big as me. He was lying on my right, and a young deer was lying on my left. I stayed as still as I could, and soon, the mountain lion got up and stood over me, looking into my eyes.

At that moment, the mountain lion, the deer, and I were not enemies, and I felt a great burden lifted from my heart. Then the big cat turned and walked into the forest. The deer stood also and walked to its mother, who was standing nearby, and they went into the forest.

Closing my eyes, I tried to make sense of what had happened and came to the conclusion that I had been dreaming. It became clear, however, that it was not a dream when I stood and looked around. The tracks of the animals left no doubt.

I returned to my family in the late afternoon. Grandmother was cooking dinner. She was very small. I lifted her in a bear hug and said, "I am sorry. Please forgive me. I love you."

She said, "I love you too, and I will love you more if you put me down and let me breathe."

I set her gently down, and she said as she straightened her clothes, "Okay, and now you are forgiven."

Bright Star, Willow's mother, cried as she forgave me and called me her son. I then went to every member of our village, including the children, and asked for their forgiveness and told them that I loved them.

Little Hawk looked at me for a very long time without saying anything. He took me into his lodge, and we sat by the fire. Lighting a bundle of sage in the fire, he looked at me again and said, "You look different, and your presence feels different. It is like you are a different person. I think I am going to miss the old Short Feather. I really liked him. What happened on the mountain?"

I told him everything, including the words written in my mind. As I told him these things, he poked the fire with a stick, but I knew he was listening carefully.

"We must talk of this again," Little Hawk said. "But now you must go to your daughter. Tell her about her mother, and tell her often until she knows what a wonderful human being Willow was."

After eating Grandmother's dinner, I took Aspen in my arms and walked a short distance into the valley. I told her about her mother. It was painful and I cried, but I loved my daughter.

Short Feather stopped and opened his eyes. Juanita's drumming stopped.

"I think this may be a good place to stop," said Short Feather. "I have more to tell, but it will have to be at another time."

Lee tenderly took Juanita's hands to help her up. He had been quiet most of the day. Everyone could tell that he had much on his mind.

Little was said on the way to Short Feather's. At Juanita's house, Lee did not go in but held Juanita and kissed her gently. He tried very hard not to show he did not want to let her go.

24

> "I have learned that love is not dependent
> on the merits of the one who is loved.
> But on the choice of the one who loves."
>
> —Short Feather

Three days later, in the afternoon, Juanita received a phone call from Allison.

"Juanita, Dr. Bronson was called to Short Feather's apartment," Allison said. "He fell, and they have taken him to the Pomona Valley Hospital."

"Oh no, how bad is it?" Juanita cried almost in a panic. "I must go there."

"I will come and get you. I'll be there as soon as I can."

When Allison arrived, Juanita was waiting out front. She had notified the men in the guard station that they should not stop Allison. Driving quickly to the hospital, both were frustrated that they did not have more information.

They walked to the emergency room. Juanita's voice was shaking as she said, "I love that old Indian so much."

"I know how you feel, sweetheart," said Allison. "In a short period of time, he has become very close and important to all of us."

Charley was in the waiting room. He stood and hugged Juanita, then Allison. "He broke his ankle. Somehow he wedged it between his bed and the nightstand. That stubborn old man got angry with me when I called your husband, Allison, and got angrier when the doctor insisted on bringing him here. I hope they give him something to make him shut up. He keeps saying he has had worse and can take care of it himself."

As Charley was speaking, Dr. Bronson walked in. Seeing Juanita's desperate look, he said, "Short Feather is in good hands, dear. They are taking x-rays now. I am afraid it may be a bad break, but his heart is strong, and he is very stubborn. I have called my sister, Dr. Abigail Cook, in Pasadena. She is the best orthopedic surgeon I know, and will be here soon."

"Do you really think it will require surgery?" asked Juanita.

"I'll know better when I see the x-rays, but I will leave the final decision up to my sister."

"When can I be with him?"

"I'll take you in as soon as he is in a room," Dr. Bronson said. "He is adamantly refusing any pain medication, saying it doesn't hurt much. It probably doesn't right now because his ankle is swollen, but we will have to get the swelling down, and then I believe he will notice it."

A nurse came and said that Dr. Cook had arrived and was looking at the x-rays. Dr. Bronson left, saying he would be back soon.

About an hour later, the same nurse came to the waiting room. Her name tag said Miss Goodyear. "The patient is in his room now. I'll take you there, but no more than two at a time can go in. There is another patient in the other bed, and he is sleeping."

Juanita and Allison went in first. Short Feather was sitting up in the hospital bed, and he had a smile but looked embarrassed. His right ankle was wrapped in ice packs, and his eagle feather was on the table next to his bed. A curtain separated the two beds.

Juanita went to one side of the bed, kissed Short Feather on the forehead, and took his hand. Allison went to the other side and did the same.

"I don't know why everyone is making such a fuss," he said. "I have been injured much worse. But, I must say, that Miss Goodyear is something else."

"Hey, that's not a good thing to say when your one true love is in the room, you old Indian," objected Juanita.

Miss Goodyear looked to be in her twenties but was actually thirty-five years old. She had blond hair, blue eyes, and was about five foot four, with a very nice figure. As she walked into the room, she asked them to be a little quieter because of the other patient.

"Oh, hell, it's okay, sweetheart," said the man in the other bed. "I'm awake, and besides, I think I know that old Indian."

The morning at Puddingstone Lake and the encounter with the biker flashed through Short Feather's mind, and he said, "Farting Horse?"

Juanita and Allison said, "Snake?" at the same time.

Miss Goodyear looked at them with a questioning look, and pushed back the curtain to reveal Snake. He had a cast on his left arm, covering his hand and continuing up his forearm, almost to his elbow. He also had a cast on his left leg, covering his foot to below his knee. It was elevated by a sling hung from a trapeze. There were also some bandages on the left side of his face. His mustache was gone, and his hair was much more conservative and shorter.

"What does your motorcycle look like?" asked Short Feather, assuming what had happened.

Snake looked like he was going to cry. "Not too good. I think it's trashed, but I was in no condition to check it out. It's a good thing I was wearing a helmet, which I usually don't. They had to throw it away. What happened to you, old man?"

"Clumsiness that comes with old age," said Short Feather.

Just then Dr. Bronson walked in with a lovely black woman. She was his sister, Dr. Abigail Cook. They were both wearing white lab coats and had stethoscopes hanging around their necks.

Allison went to the woman and gave her a hug. "Abigail, thank you for coming. It is so good to have you here."

"Allison, would you please get Charley and Lee so that we don't have to explain everything twice?" asked Dr. Bronson.

Juanita was very glad that Lee had arrived.

Dr. Cook went to Short Feather, took his pulse, and listened to his heart. She was very professional and, after checking the chart, said, looking at Short Feather, "You are one hundred and ten years old." It was not a question.

When everyone was in the room, Dr. Cook went on. "I am going to tell it to you straight. Surgery is dangerous at any age, but at your age, we can multiply the danger by one hundred and ten. If I do not do surgery and put the bones back together with pins and screws, you will be in a wheelchair and on pain medication for the rest of your life. If I do the surgery and you survive, you will be in a wheelchair for at least eight weeks, and I don't think you will ever walk normally again. It is up to you and your family. Do you have any questions?"

Short Feather took Dr. Cook's hand and, looking into her eyes, said with a smile, "I have not walked normally for over twenty years, whatever normal is. You will do the surgery. How long will I be in this hospital room?"

"The length of your hospitalization will depend on your recovery and cooperation, but at least ten days," the doctor responded.

"How long will Farting Horse be here?"

"Who?" asked a surprised Dr. Cook.

"He means me, lady," said Snake from the other bed. "And my doctor said at least ten more days."

"Good," said Short Feather. "That will motivate me to cooperate and recover more quickly."

"Likewise," mumbled Snake.

Short Feather still held Dr. Cook's hand. "Will I be able to go home?"

"You will need to go to a care facility unless you have someone at home who can take care of you."

Juanita spoke up quickly. "He will have me. I can take care of him, and I have already talked to a friend about taking over my cleaning business so that I can start school in the fall. I am sure she would not mind starting right away."

"I will back Juanita up," said Charley. "Plus we have Mrs. Watson upstairs."

"Good," said Dr. Cook, turning to Short Feather. "I will see you in the morning. If your leg begins to hurt too much, Miss Goodyear will give you something for the pain. Just let her know."

"It's pretty good stuff," said Snake. "I just floated off into the sunset."

Dr. Bronson and Dr. Cook left. Allison went with them.

Soon after the doctors left, there was a commotion in the hallway, and Miss Goodyear came into the room. "A very pushy man says he is the patient's great-grandson. He looks old enough to be his brother. Should I let him in?"

"I heard that," said Edward Conrad as he barged into the room. "And, of course, you should let me in."

"This *is* my great-grandson, Nurse." Short Feather sighed. "I am sorry he is so pushy."

Edward went to the opposite side of the bed from Juanita, who was still holding Short Feather's hand. Miss Goodyear left the room.

"Now what have you done, old man?" asked Edward, looking at the ankle wrapped in ice packs. "This is going to cost you a fortune and reduce my inheritance."

"Ha!" said Short Feather. "You try to act like all you care about is money, but I know you give away most of what you earn. I think it is funny that Miss Goodyear said you looked my age."

Edward laughed. "I think she likes me, and you said *Miss Goodyear*? Maybe I should take her out to dinner. I like people who are not afraid to stand up to me. If there is anything you need, Grandfather, let me know. I have to go."

Edward Conrad left as quickly as he had arrived.

"What was that, a tornado?" asked Snake.

"My great-grandson," said Short Feather, laughing. "He means well."

Miss Goodyear came into the room, carrying a white paper cup. "Here are your pills, Henry." She handed the cup to Snake.

"Close the curtain, will you, Nurse? These make me sleepy, and I need a nap," said Snake—Henry.

Juanita and Short Feather looked at each other and whispered at the same time, "Henry?"

Charley and Lee were standing against the wall. Charley looked confused.

"I am feeling tired," said Short Feather, "and I want to tell more of my story before I have surgery. I will need my drum, and it is at home."

"Oooooh, my god," came from the other side of the curtain.

"I will not bother anyone with it. I just need to have it with me," said Short Feather in an appealing way.

Again, from the other side of the curtain, "Kind of like a teddy bear?"

"I'm going off duty now," said Miss Goodyear. "I have a dinner date. If you need anything, just push your button and Mrs. Gunderson will come."

Lee said to Short Feather, "Charley and I will go and get your drum. Is there anything else you need, Grandfather? We will need a key."

"Yes, please bring my Bible."

More groans came from the other side of the curtain.

"And Mrs. Watson, upstairs in 17, has a key. She will be worried. Please tell her I am fine and she should not try to visit until tomorrow."

Lee and Charley left, after Lee kissed Juanita.

Juanita continued to hold Short Feather's hand in both of hers. Soon, he was sound asleep. It was 5:00 p.m.

25

> "It is better to find out who and what a person really is before misjudging them and casting them aside."
>
> —Short Feather

Dr. Cook and Dr. Bronson, sister and brother, were looking again at the x-rays and talking about Short Feather's surgery. The anesthesiologist, Dr. Rand, was there.

Dr. Rand looked very concerned. "The patient is one hundred and ten years old. I don't like this. We all know the odds."

"Yes," said Dr. Cook. "This is not a surgery I look forward to. There are so many things that can go wrong before, during, and after. The positives are, however, that he has a strong heart and a good attitude. He clearly understands the dangers. I could tell he had no misgivings when he looked into my eyes. I will have my usual assistant, and Dr. Bronson will be there to help monitor. I have reserved OR2 for 10:00 a.m."

She went on to describe the procedure in detail.

At exactly 5:30 p.m., Mrs. Gunderson came into the room and said with a loud and authoritative voice, "Well! Why have these patients not ordered dinner?"

Juanita jumped, and Short Feather's eyes opened wide. Mrs. Gunderson was short and stout. Short Feather thought she looked like Nikita Khrushchev with hair and wearing a dress, but he kept that to himself.

Roughly pushing the curtain back, Mrs. Gunderson said, "Come on, Mr. Ott, the menu is right next to you on the table. Just mark what you want, and I'll take care of it. You too, Mr. Feather."

Juanita chuckled.

"I'm not hungry," whined Snake. "Can't you just leave me alone?"

"I don't care if you eat it. My job is to see that you get it. I'll be right back." Mrs. Gunderson left the room.

"She sure reminds me of someone, but I can't think who it is," said Snake, as he fumbled with the pencil and paper.

Short Feather looked at the menu. Nothing looked really good, but there was meat loaf with mashed potatoes and gravy. *How far wrong can you go with that?* he thought to himself.

"I wonder if I can get a chocolate milkshake," said Short Feather.

Snake held up the menu. "There is a line at the bottom that says 'Requests.' What are you getting to eat?"

"He is getting the meat loaf," said Juanita, as she went to help Snake. He was having trouble marking the paper with just one hand, and he wanted a chocolate shake too.

"Thank you, Juanita," said Snake.

She said, "You're welcome, Henry Ott."

Short Feather chuckled.

"Khrushchev," said Snake. "That's who she reminds me of—Khrushchev."

Lee and Charley arrived back at the room about the same time that dinner arrived. Lee placed Short Feather's drum and Bible on the table and said, "Charley and I are going to take Juanita to the cafeteria for dinner while you boys eat."

Juanita looked at Lee and said, "I don't want to leave him."

"You go ahead, my little Buffalo Tail," said Short Feather. "We will be fine. We have Nikita—I mean, Mrs. Gunderson."

Just after Lee, Charley, and Juanita left the room, Snake questioned between mouthfuls, "Buffalo Tail?"

When Lee, Charley, and Juanita returned about forty-five minutes later, Short Feather and Snake were laughing about something, although both looked like laughing was painful.

Mrs. Gunderson came in carrying a portable tape recorder. Setting it on the table next to Short Feather and plugging it in, she said, "Dr. Bronson said he and his wife cannot be here, and you will know what to do with this." And she left.

There were two guest chairs for each bed. Charley borrowed one from Snake, and they all sat down. Juanita was on Short Feather's right as before. He was hooked up to an IV on his left. He could use his left hand, but it was awkward.

"Buffalo Tail, please put my drum next to me on the bed," said Short Feather. "I believe my story has me with my new family somewhere in Colorado in 1876."

Charley turned on the tape recorder. Short Feather closed his eyes and began to lightly tap the drum. It could hardly be heard because the bed deadened the sound.

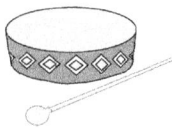

We spent that winter in the same valley. It was peaceful and quiet, but all of us had to be on constant alert. Lookouts were posted day and night. Hunting and taking care of all the chores that life demanded kept everyone busy.

Little Hawk and I spent much time together talking and trying to figure out what the future would bring. Sometimes we would talk about my spiritual experience on the mountain.

One long, cold winter night, Little Hawk said, "I hope you don't mind, but I have talked to Black Bear about you. He is old and wise and has given me great insight and advice. I think I know the meaning of what happened to you."

"Please tell me," I said. "I have some ideas, but I want to know what you think."

Little Hawk lit some sage at the fire. This was always pleasing. "First, you were prevented from walking over the cliff to your death. Obviously, it means that you were meant to live, but I think it also means that you will live a long life. I arrived at this after putting it together with the rest.

"Next, the Great Spirit revealed to you that all human beings must be considered to be his children and you must learn to love them. Amazingly he also revealed that whites are human beings. I still struggle with this. Surely Chivington and his band cannot be considered human beings. How could we ever learn to love them after Sand Creek?"

I thought about this for a moment. "Willow used to say, 'It is easy to love those who love you. The real test of one's character is when one can love those who are bad and do hateful things.' I believe I am learning that love is not dependent on the merits of the one who is loved but on the choice of the one who loves."

"These ideas are difficult," said Little Hawk. "Willow seemed to understand so easily, and yet she was eager to fight and kill those she said we should love."

"Willow would fiercely defend her family against anything or anyone who threatened it. Even those she loved," I said with conviction.

"I will have to think on these things further," said Little Hawk. "But we must consider the mountain lion and the young deer. I believe the mountain lion represents the white nation and the young deer represents Indians—all Indians of every tribe. The fact that you lay between them tells me that you will be a mediator, as you have already been. I think that what you do will never be well-known, but it will have great and lasting effects."

"My brother, I thank you for your wisdom," I stated. "I will consider what you have said, and we must talk again, but now I must go to my daughter and tell her about her mother. I tell her every night, even if she is asleep."

Short Feather stopped and grimaced.
"Are you all right, Grandfather?" asked Juanita.
"I think the swelling is going down. The ankle is hurting more, but talking to you helps. I hope I am not bothering Snake too much."
Snake said nothing, but Juanita could tell he had been listening.
"Should we call for the nurse?" asked Juanita. "She could give you something for the pain."
Short Feather shifted in the bed a little. "Not yet. It will put me to sleep, and I do not want to sleep yet."
Lee spoke up. "Grandfather, may I ask you a question?"
"Of course, White Tears, what do you want to know?"
"You talk about learning to love all of God's children, yet you almost did not allow me into your home when we first met. I have seen you be kind to many white people, even Snake, but you profess to dislike white people."
Short Feather held up his hand to stop Lee. "I have found, White Tears, that sometimes it is helpful to maintain an image that may not be totally accurate. With the white world, I was Ken, the 'big, dumb' Indian. I am an angry Indian with my Indian brothers and sisters. They come to me on occasion for counsel and advice. Most are very suspicious of the white man, many are full of hate.

They are more open with me and listen better when they believe that I feel the same way. They do not come around much anymore. They think that at one hundred and ten I am senile, or should be. Sometimes I am, and that has also been helpful."

"Thank you, Grandfather, I think I understand," said Lee with a smile.

Short Feather closed his eyes and began gently tapping the drum.

Our small group of families stayed together under the leadership of Little Hawk. Life was not easy, but we were happy, and hardly ever saw the Long Knives. Continuing to gradually move south with the intention of joining other Southern Cheyenne, we did hear of the plight of the many tribes. Most were now on reservations with few options other than to be totally dependent on the US government, which was not very sympathetic or honest. We did not want any part of that, so we stayed small and out of the way, avoiding any contact with whites.

Grandmother died in the winter of 1877-78. This was hard on all of us. She was an amazing woman, and greatly loved. I will never forget her wisdom, love, and dedication to her family. Aspen was not yet two, and for the next few months, she kept looking for Grandmother to come into our lodge.

In the spring of 1879, Little Hawk and I concluded that we needed some white man tools that could make our lives easier. Shovels, picks, and axes had become essential. The few we started out with were badly worn or broken. I had been teaching the white man's tongue to the village, but because I spoke and understood it best, it was decided I would travel to a trading post that was about a five-day trip. The proprietor was said to be friendly to the Indians.

Bright Star, Aspen, and Little Hawk's son, Sky Hawk, would go with me.

Aspen was now almost three years old and into everything. I wanted her with me, no matter what. We dressed in our oldest and most ragged clothing and took deer, elk, bear, and other skins to trade. We had my mule, Left Alone, along with three ponies and a packhorse. We would not take the ponies near the trading post, of course.

Traveling was not difficult. We stayed away from the main roads as well as the farms and ranches that now dotted the land. Aspen mainly rode with me and was constantly pointing out the birds and animals that we saw. She was bright and happy with everything, just like her mother, and made the miles and time fly by. When there was time, I taught Sky Hawk how to shoot without ever firing a shot—just as Thunderstorm had taught me.

Short Feather grimaced again and stopped drumming. "I am afraid that I must stop. The pain is becoming unbearable. I am so sorry, my children, I have so much more to tell."

Charley and Lee stood and went to the side of the bed. Charley turned off the tape recorder, and Juanita took Short Feather's hand in both of hers after laying the drum aside.

Lee pushed the call button. "It is okay, Grandfather, you will have plenty of time to tell us more after the surgery."

"Yes, of course," said Short Feather. "I have faced many more dangerous…" His voice trailed off as he grimaced again.

Mrs. Gunderson came in quickly. "I was wondering how long you could do without this pain medication," she said as she injected it into the IV.

"It is a good thing that is what I wanted," said Short Feather. "You never asked and what if I just needed to…."

Short Feather drifted off into the sunset, just like Snake said he would.

Mrs. Gunderson huffed in a surly way and left the room.

Juanita said with great emotion, "I don't know what I will do if he doesn't make it. I don't want to lose him."

Mrs. Gunderson came back to say in a much nicer way, "It is time for visitors to leave. Surgery is scheduled for 10:00 a.m. You can come back at eight. He will be fine. I'll take good care of him."

"Me too," said Snake. "And don't worry. I know he will be okay."

Juanita, Lee, and Charley left reluctantly.

26

"Friends are the greatest of treasure."

—Ruth Gale

At 7:00 a.m., Dr. Bronson and Dr. Cook were standing over Short Feather. Dr. Cook was listening to Short Feather's heart and taking his pulse. Dr. Bronson was looking at the chart.

"I heard him moan a few times in the night," said Snake from the other side of the curtain. "I pushed the button for the nurse. She gave him some more of the good stuff."

Dr. Bronson pushed back the curtain. "Yes, I see that on the chart. Thank you, Snake."

"He will be okay, won't he?" asked Snake. "I told Juanita he would be, and I want to hear more of his story."

"I do too," said Dr. Bronson. "He is very old, and as you well know, this can be hard on a young person. It is, however, good to keep a positive attitude, and I appreciate yours."

"I'm sorry I called you a nigger in the park that day. For the first time in my life, I am ashamed of myself," said Snake with a sincerity that was not lost on Dr. Bronson.

"You are forgiven," replied Dr. Bronson. "It appears I misjudged you also."

Short Feather seemed to have slept through it all but had a slight smile on his face.

At 8:00 a.m. on the dot, Juanita and Lee walked into the hospital room. They had a matronly woman with them who looked very concerned. She was Mrs. Watson, Short Feather's neighbor. Charley had stayed home to watch her miniature schnauzer, Oskar.

Short Feather was awake, but groggy. Juanita and Mrs. Watson stood on opposite sides of the bed and took his hands.

"It is nice to have two of my favorite women so concerned about me," said Short Feather with as much of a smile that he could muster. "But you should not worry. I will be fine. How are you, Grace, and how is Oskar?"

Grace wiped a tear. "Oh, my dear friend, I am good, and Oskar always does well as long as he gets his walks and cookies."

Lee brought chairs for the women, and Miss Goodyear came in to get Snake's breakfast order.

At 9:00 a.m., the anesthesiologist, Dr. Rand, arrived and asked everyone to wait in the hallway. He was with Short Feather for about ten minutes, and when he left, he did not look at anyone or say anything. Miss Goodyear told the three that they would need to go to the OR waiting room on the second floor.

"Dr. Bronson said he would see you when the surgery is completed," she added. "He estimates it will take about three hours."

Allison was already in the waiting room when Lee, Juanita, and Grace arrived. Edward Conrad and Allison's baby, Breeze, were also there. In fact, Edward was holding Breeze on his lap and reading a book to her. She seemed to enjoy watching his face more than looking at the pictures. Edward acknowledged their presence as he continued reading to Breeze.

"She took to him right away, just like she did with Short Feather," said an amazed Allison while looking at Edward.

At 1:30 p.m., Dr. Bronson came into the waiting room. He had a big smile and said, "Short Feather is in recovery, ICU. Everything

went well. We are all amazed. Abby, Dr. Cook said that it was like he was helping with the surgery. Dr. Rand said that he had never seen anything like it. He said, 'The patient was anesthetized, seemed to be aware of what was going on, and yet was somewhere else.' I don't know what either of them meant. They will have to explain. I did observe that Short Feather seemed to be in control."

"How long will he be in recovery?" asked Lee.

"It all looks so good I think he will be back in his room in time to order dinner."

Juanita and Grace asked at the same time, "Can we see him?"

"He will be out for a while longer," said Dr. Bronson. "Why don't we all go and get some lunch? Just let me change, and I'll be right out."

Lee left immediately to get Charley. Grace said that Oskar would be just fine alone for an hour or two. They agreed to meet at a small Mexican restaurant, which was Dr. Bronson's favorite. Juanita said that the food was okay but her enchiladas were much better. Lee said Juanita would need to make enchiladas for them so they could compare. Everyone agreed.

Grace talked about Short Feather and how much he meant to her. "My husband, Frank, passed away suddenly last year. I was totally lost when it came to my finances. Frank had always handled them. I did not even know what bank he used. Short Feather got it all straightened out and showed me what to do. Edward handled the legal stuff. I could not be more grateful."

Juanita asked, "Why didn't Short Feather give you an Indian name?"

"Oh, but he did," responded Grace. "He calls me Amazing Grace because I play hymns all the time on my stereo. I insisted that he just call me Grace. My real name is Rhonda."

Edward Conrad was still taking care of Breeze, feeding her some rice but definitely no beans, as Allison had insisted.

Lee asked Dr. Bronson, "You said earlier that during the surgery Short Feather seemed to be in control. What did you mean?"

"I was monitoring his vitals," replied Dr. Bronson. "Usually a nurse will do that, but I really wanted to be there. At one point, his blood pressure started to drop. I mentioned this to the other doctors, heard what sounded like a grunt from Short Feather, and by the time I looked again, it was normal."

"Don't ever underestimate that old Indian," said Edward, as Breeze threw some rice at him.

By 3:00 p.m., Short Feather was back in the room. He was hungry, so Snake ordered chocolate shakes for both of them. Miss Goodyear said that would be okay. Juanita and Grace arrived at the same time as the shakes were delivered. They told Short Feather and Snake about lunch, and both groaned with envy.

"Next to pizza, my favorite food is Mexican," said Snake.

Short Feather looked over at him and smiled. "It is amazing how much we have in common, Farting Horse."

Lee took Charley back to Oskar. Allison took Breeze home, and Edward was in the hall talking to Miss Goodyear as she cleaned the rice and stains from his tie. They seemed to be getting along quite well.

"How are you doing, you old Indian?" asked Juanita. "I was worried sick."

Short Feather took another sip of his shake. "Actually, I feel quite good, but would you please try to find out how that little girl is doing?"

"What little girl is that?" asked Dr. Cook as she walked into the room.

"The one that was on the gurney next to mine while I was waiting to go into surgery," answered Short Feather.

Dr. Cook looked confused and a little alarmed. "I don't see how you could have known about her. Dr. Rand had already put you under."

"Lydia was frightened, and we had a nice talk. I took her to a beautiful meadow with a stream flowing through it. She picked flowers with an older woman that she called Gran. How is she?" asked Short Feather.

Dr. Cook reluctantly answered, "I am afraid she never made it to surgery. It was a bad accident. Now please, I need to see how *you* are doing."

Finishing, Dr. Cook said, "Amazingly, you are doing quite well, and it is a good sign that you are still with us in spite of Dr. Rand's predictions. You are not out of the woods, so I want you to do exactly what the nurse and Dr. Bronson tell you to do."

As Dr. Cook was leaving, Short Feather said, "Thank you, Bone Mender. You were amazing in surgery. I could not have asked for better."

The doctor looked at Juanita with a questioning smile. Juanita shrugged, and the doctor left.

Lee returned with Charley at about 6:00 p.m. He and Juanita took Grace home, met Oskar, and then went out to dinner. Lee chose a small, quiet, out-of-the-way restaurant.

⁂

When Lee and Juanita returned, they found Short Feather, Charley, and Mrs. Gunderson laughing at a story that Snake was telling.

"That is quite an experience you had, Mr. Ott," said the nurse as she left the room.

Charley stood, looked at Lee then Juanita, and started grinning ear to ear, but said nothing. Juanita went to Short Feather, kissed him on the forehead, and then took his hand.

Short Feather got a sly smile on his face. "Well, when is the wedding?"

Juanita blushed. "Oh, you sneaky old Indian, how did you know? Lee only just asked me."

"That is quite a ring on your finger, my little Buffalo Tail. Did you really think I would not notice? Besides, I knew it was only a matter of time."

"We decided to wait until you can walk her down the aisle, Grandfather," said Lee. "So I hope you heal quickly."

"I could not be more pleased," said Short Feather. "I will do my best, but now I need some rest."

"That's pretty good, you made a rhyme," said Snake.

Everyone laughed.

Mrs. Gunderson came in to say that visiting hours were over.

The next day was Saturday. Lee, Juanita, and Charley arrived at the hospital at 8:00 a.m. A different nurse was helping Short Feather to sit in a wheelchair. It was painful for him to lower his cast leg, but the pain only lasted for a moment.

Snake was not in the room. He had been taken to see if he was able to use crutches. The nurse left instructions that Short Feather was to stay in the chair until his bed could be changed. She adjusted the chair so that his cast leg was elevated and stuck straight out.

"Let's go for a walk," said Lee. "I'll push."

Charley took charge of the IV stand as they walked through the halls of the hospital. They were stopped by attendants, nurses, and even two doctors. They all said something like, "Are you the man with the broken ankle? You're one hundred and ten years old—amazing!"

Arriving back at the room, they found Snake in a chair with a pair of crutches next to him. There was a well-dressed large man sitting with him who looked vaguely familiar. His suit looked expensive and fit him like it was made just for him. His tie was silk, and he even had cuff links that were clearly gold.

"Short Feather, Juanita, Lee, you probably do not recognize Hugo from the park," said Snake with a funny smile.

Hugo got up and shook hands with everyone. "I never really got to meet you at the park. Snake was being his usual self. My actual name is Hugh Westgate."

Lee looked confused. "You're one of the other bikers at the park. You sure don't look like a biker now."

"No, Henry and I and a few other businessmen only ride on some weekends. The rest of the time I take care of my women's clothing store in Beverly Hills." Hugh was well-spoken. "I love motorcycles, and becoming a totally different person on weekends has kept me from getting ulcers. Henry owns four auto parts stores in Southern California and two in the San Francisco Bay Area."

"Well, if you are going to talk about me, I'm leaving," said Snake. "One of the benefits of being able to use crutches is that I can go to the bathroom on my own."

When the door closed, Hugh turned to Short Feather. "I don't know what you did or said to Henry that day in the park, but he has been a totally different person. We were all worried about him. He was taking the outlaw biker thing way too seriously, but since then, he has been nice to everybody. Thank you."

"Grandfather certainly does have a way with people," said Juanita.

Short Feather asked, "How did he wreck his bike?"

"Swerved to miss hitting a dog, ended up wrapping his bike around a tree," answered Hugh.

Snake came back and climbed into bed with difficulty, but refused help.

"I need to leave now," said Hugh. "One of my salesgirls is getting married, and I don't want to miss the wedding. She is a nice kid, and I really like her fiancé."

Short Feather reached for his drum. Lee and Charley found chairs, and Charley turned on the tape recorder.

27

"Sometimes we say and do stupid things. We should not be too hard on ourselves. But learn from our mistakes."

—Buckskin

"I believe my story was at the point where Bright Star, Sky Hawk, Aspen, and I were on our way to the trading post. We needed tools for our village." Closing his eyes, Short Feather began tapping his drum.

We camped about two miles away from the trading post in a secluded area. Early the next morning, I took Aspen and Left Alone, loaded with the skins and furs, and headed toward the store. Bright Star and Sky Hawk stayed with the ponies. The only weapons I took were my bow with a few arrows and my knife.

Arriving at the trading post, John Gale's Store, I scanned the area. There was a horse with a saddle and a packhorse tied up to the rail. Near the corral, which had many horses, was a mountain man in fringed buckskin pants and shirt, and even a coonskin cap. He was not a big man, and had a horse, a mule, and a dog. The mule was loaded with supplies. Aspen and I had to walk past them to get to the store.

Aspen pointed at the dog and started to walk toward it. The dog was wagging its tail.

The man jumped up, grabbed the dog, and yelled at me in poor Cheyenne, "Get back, stay away." Then in English, "Keep that filthy nit away from my dog. I don't want my dog getting its stinkin' lice and fleas."

Then he said to himself, "I don't know why they still let those savages walk around loose on our land."

I said nothing, picked up Aspen, and kept walking. After tying Left Alone to a post away from the horses, we headed for the store. I had told Aspen that she should not speak any English at the trading post. I told her again.

Aspen wanted down when we walked through the front door. I stopped just inside and held her hand. Not wanting to be too forward, I waited until the proprietor was finished with his customer. The customer was a big man who was clearly not happy to see Indians there. I could tell that by the way he looked at us. When he was finished at the counter, he walked toward me carrying a brand-new rifle and stopped right in front of me. He was almost as big as me, and we looked into each other's eyes. I stepped aside with Aspen even though there was plenty of room for him to exit; he walked out of the store.

The proprietor, John Gale, still behind the counter, motioned for me to come forward. He asked, "Cheyenne?" I nodded yes. He asked what I needed. His Cheyenne was not very good, but much better than that of the mountain man. I did not speak but pointed to the shovels, picks, and axes. He came from behind the counter. "What have you got to trade?"

Just then a woman came from the back of the store. She was obviously John's wife—about the same age, maybe late forties or early fifties. Her hair was totally white and done up on the top of her head. John was almost bald. She was wearing a blue calico dress that almost reached to the floor and a white apron.

When the woman saw Aspen, she got a big smile, wiped her hands on her apron, and said, "Oh, look at that darlin' little child." She got down on her knees, opened her arms, and cooed, "Here, child, come to Aunt Ruth."

Aspen ran to her, and they embraced. This surprised and concerned me greatly. Aspen did seem to love everybody and was way too trusting, but at three years old, she had plenty of time to learn about people.

John saw my concern and said, "They will be okay. Ruth loves all children. We never had any of our own."

"I am sorry," I said. We were still speaking in Cheyenne. I did not want him to know I spoke English. "I need the tools for my people who are in the mountains."

John and I went out to Left Alone and brought in the furs and skins. Ruth was giving Aspen a piece of candy—the first Aspen had ever had—and her eyes went wide. John looked through the furs and skins. Then he gathered up three shovels, two picks, two axes, and a sharpening tool. I could not have been happier but tried hard not to show it.

John watched my face then turned around and walked to a shelf behind the counter. He came back with a can labeled "Lemon Drops" and placed it with the other items.

Ruth came forward with a spool of red ribbon and cut off a long piece. Skillfully making a bow, she somehow attached it to Aspen's hair and held up a mirror. Aspen grinned from ear to ear and squealed. Ruth put the spool of red ribbon next to the lemon drops.

Turning to her husband, Ruth said quietly, "John, this little girl speaks English. She cannot be much more than three years old. She certainly looks Cheyenne. Do you think she could have been taken from a mission or school?"

I pretended to not understand what was said. It was difficult.

John looked carefully at me again and said to Ruth, "I think we need to notify the Indian agent."

I decided that it was time to speak up, "Aspen is my daughter. I taught her to speak English as well as most of the people of my village. Her mother was killed by the Long Knives at the Battle of the Greasy Grass."

John and Ruth looked at me with their mouths open until John said, "Custer's last stand?"

"Yes," I said.

"How did you learn to speak English so well?" asked Ruth.

I hesitated but decided to tell them. "A wonderful woman named Maggie Lawson taught me and also taught me to read and write."

John and Ruth looked at each other and both said at the same time, "You are Short Feather!"

John came quickly forward and shook my hand. Ruth actually grabbed me in a bear hug and said, "Poor Maggie has been so worried about you. She thought you might have been killed. She has heard nothing since she got a letter from a Sergeant Worthington in the Seventh Cavalry over four years ago. He told her that you saved his life and took him back to his unit. Then she found out later that the sergeant had been killed at the Little Bighorn. He was with Major Reno."

While she was saying this, John went behind the counter and was looking through a drawer. He came back with a sealed envelope and handed it to me. On the front, it said in Maggie's written Cheyenne, "Short Feather."

"I have had this for almost two and a half years. Maggie gives one of these to anyone that might have a chance of running into you. I never thought it would be Ruth and me," said John with a big smile. "Now you read your letter. I will get together some more things for you, and I know Ruth will love to spend more time with Aspen."

I went outside and opened the envelope. Inside was a short letter written in Maggie's Cheyenne. There was no date.

My dearest Short Feather,

Please come home. We all miss you very much and are very concerned. Do not think that you will not be welcomed. I think I will know when you are reading this letter.

Love,
Maggie

This was typical for Maggie: short and to the point, with an interesting last sentence. I read the letter a few more times and sat for a while, thinking about it.

When I went back into the store, John was putting flour, beans, coffee, and other items into a flour sack. Ruth was putting a new hat onto Aspen's head and a scarf around her neck.

I said, "This is all too much. The skins and furs are not worth that much."

John just looked at me. "Short Feather, I just can't believe it is you. Maggie will be so happy when we see her next month." He stood up, as if he had just had a great idea and said enthusiastically, "Why don't you and Aspen come with us? By the way, are you two alone, or did others come with you?"

"Aspen's grandmother and a boy are waiting for us in a hidden place." I decided to be totally honest with these white people. "They are taking care of our ponies."

"It is good that you did not bring the ponies here. There are many people that do not feel the same as us about Indians. They would not like seeing you with ponies." John went on thoughtfully, "Now listen, Ruth and I will be going to Dodge City in a little over a month. It is our regular trip for supplies, and we take three wagons. I usually hire two men to drive the other wagons. I'll just hire you and one other man. You can drive a wagon?"

"Yes, I can," I said hesitantly. I was beginning to feel overwhelmed. There was much to think about. "I must think about this. My village is my family, and I will not leave my wife's mother. Thank you for your offer. When must I let you know my decision?"

"If you show up before we leave, that is all the notice I need."

John helped me load the supplies onto Left Alone. Soon, Ruth brought out Aspen, who was holding a small book.

"Now, sweetheart, you have your papa read that to you every night," instructed Ruth.

It was the New Testament of the Bible. Part of the same book Maggie had read.

Short Feather stopped for a drink of water. Miss Goodyear was checking the IV but left quickly when she heard a buzzer.

"You were at that massacre?" asked Snake.

"Yes," answered Short Feather. "There were many people killed on both sides."

"Wow, sorry about your wife."

"It was a long time ago."

Short Feather closed his eyes, and the drumming continued. The tape recorder was still running.

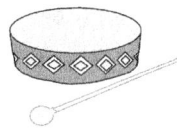

Aspen, Left Alone, and I found Bright Star and Sky Hawk doing quite well and preparing our midday meal. It was a warm day, and the sun was now directly overhead. After eating, I decided that we should start toward home since we had many hours of daylight left. Again, we stayed off the main road.

After a few hours, we came to a meadow with a stream running through it. I saw a horse grazing. It was saddled, and even had a rifle in its holder on the side. This was definitely unusual. With Sky Hawk's help, I managed to grab hold of the reins and realized it was the horse belonging to the mountain man we had seen at the trading post.

Following the horse's tracks was not difficult, but it had run a great distance. When the sun was getting lower in the west, I found two sets of tracks. One set showed the horse running out of a small canyon, and the other indicated it carried a rider going into the canyon. We also found the tracks of a mule and a dog.

I decided to have Bright Star, Sky Hawk, and Aspen wait with our ponies and Left Alone in the forest. I would go into the canyon alone. I left my rifle and six-shooter with Sky Hawk; both were loaded.

Proceeding into the canyon and following the tracks, I soon came to a rocky area. The first thing I saw was the dog. There was much blood, and it was dead. Just beyond the dog was the mule, and it was also dead, with chunks of meat ripped from its left hindquarter. There was a downed tree lying on the rocks, and as I got closer, I heard moaning. In the rocks, close to the tree trunk was the mountain man. He had blood on his face, and his right leg was wedged between the trunk and a large boulder. I could tell immediately that his leg was broken and he could not move.

The man looked at me through half-closed eyes and said with a raspy voice, "Why don't you have a gun, you big dumb Injun? That beast is right behind you."

I turned around slowly and found that I was staring into the eyes of the biggest mountain lion I had ever seen. Even bigger than the one I had seen on the mountain. It was about ten feet away, standing on the end of the downed tree. Not moving, it just stood there looking into my eyes.

I drew my knife and said in Cheyenne, "I do not want to hurt you."

The cat stayed where it was and just watched me as I walked cautiously to the mule. After cutting off the right hindquarter, with some difficulty, I put the meat on a rock near the cat and said, "Take this and leave, my brother. We are not enemies at this time."

The cat looked at me for a long time, picked up the meat, and started to walk away. Then it stopped and looked back at me one last time. The look in his eyes was just like that of Little Hawk when he said to Sergeant Worthington, "If I ever see you again, I will kill you."

Snake was chuckling. Short feather stopped drumming and opened his eyes.

"That's quite a yarn," said Snake. "Do you really think that cat understood Cheyenne?"

Short Feather also chuckled. "Yes, it is an unbelievable story, but every word is true." He paused and took another drink of water. "No, I do not believe the cat understood Cheyenne, but he clearly understood the tone of my voice and the look in my eyes, just as I understood him. Communication does not always require words."

"Sorry I interrupted," said Snake. "What happened next?"

Short Feather continued.

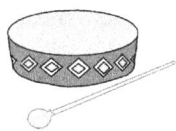

It was difficult and painful for the man, but I did manage to free his leg without doing more damage. When he passed out, everything became easier, and I placed him in the only shade I could find behind a large boulder. There was a canteen of water on the dead mule with the other supplies.

I dampened a cloth and cleaned the blood from the man's face. He had a small gash and a large bump on his forehead. When he came to, I was looking around and found what I was looking for. His six-shooter had fallen among the rocks where he could not get to it. When I handed his gun to him, he looked at me like I was crazy.

"I will be back," I said in Cheyenne, and ran to the opening of the canyon where I could see the place where I had left my family. They came out of the trees and headed toward me when they saw my signal.

Sky Hawk and I made a travois while Bright Star tended to the man's leg and head. No words were spoken between them, but he was clearly grateful. We attached the travois to the man's horse and made a platform on it for him to lie on. After loading his supplies onto his horse, we were ready to travel, but the man insisted that we take his dead dog to bury later. I wrapped it in one of his blankets, and he held the body in his arms. When that was done, we quickly got ready to leave. I did not want to be in that spot when the mountain lion returned.

With the man settled on the travois, I asked in English, "What is your name?"

"You speak English," he said, surprised. "Why didn't you say so?"

"I had my reasons. What is your name?" I asked again.

"Stephen Aloysius Gregory," he said, grimacing and putting his hand on his leg. "But you can call me Buckskin."

"I am Short Feather," I said.

As I walked away, I heard him mumble, "Dumb name."

Sky Hawk led Buckskin's horse at the front of our caravan. I stayed in the rear. Aspen rode with me except when she rode with Sky Hawk, which she seemed to prefer. We headed for our village. I figured that the slower pace with the travois would add at least two days to our trip.

"Okay, okay," said Snake. "I give up. What is a travois?"

Short Feather laughed. "Does anyone know?"

Juanita and Lee shrugged.

Charley said, "I believe it is two long poles with a cross piece forming a triangle that is dragged behind a horse, a dog, or even a man."

"You are correct," said Short Feather.

Dr. Cook came into the room. She was holding a picture of an elementary school class with about thirty children.

She said, "Short Feather, please look at this picture."

Short Feather looked at the picture for a few seconds and said in a low, quiet voice, "Oh, look, there is Lydia in the second row, four in from the left."

Dr. Cook had to find a place to sit down. Looking dizzy and a little shocked, she sat on Snake's bed, staring at Short Feather. Miss Goodyear came in and asked if the doctor was all right. She had never seen a doctor sit on a patient's bed.

"I am fine," answered Dr. Cook as she stood, and her words began to spill out. "Short Feather, Lydia's parents are grieving, but they are also very strong. Their faith in God is unshaken despite the tragedy that has befallen them. I told them what you said about being with Lydia, and they want to visit with you. Lydia's grandmother passed away about a year ago, and Lydia called her Gran. This picture is of her fourth-grade class, she was ten years old. There is no way you could have known what she looked like. Her head and face were heavily bandaged. I just don't understand. Would it be okay if they came to visit?"

"Yes, of course," said Short Feather quietly and with great concern. "I would love to meet them, but alone. It must be just me and them."

"I will bring them later today," said Dr. Cook, as she took the photograph and left.

Everyone in the room was quiet and looking at Short Feather. He said, "She was such a beautiful, happy child."

The tape recorder was still running. Charley turned it off.

Short Feather looked at his family and said, "I think I need to rest for a while."

28

"Do not be afraid of dying. Pay attention to how you live."

—Short Feather

Lee and Juanita took Charley home so that he could take care of Oskar for Grace. She was ready to go but said that another neighbor had begged for Oskar. Everyone loved the little dog, and Charley did not have to stay to take care of him. Lee treated them to lunch at a little café near the telephone office where he worked.

Arriving back at the hospital, the four found Short Feather trying to summarize his story to get Snake caught up. It was not easy because Snake asked so many questions.

"I think Farting Horse and I will have plenty of time to get all of his questions answered," said Short Feather.

"Are you really going to keep calling me that?" questioned Snake.

Short Feather looked confused. "Why would I not? It is your name, after all."

Snake sighed.

Short Feather gave Grace a condensed version of the part she had missed. She said she wanted to hear the earlier part on the tape later. Charley turned the recorder on. Short Feather closed his eyes and began tapping the drum.

After we had gone a few miles, we stopped to bury the dog. I placed Buckskin by the grave, and the man actually cried. Little Aspen stood next to him, holding his hand and softly crying with him. That scene is burned into my mind.

Having an injured man did slow us down considerably. Buckskin, however, was not a complainer and did not demand constant attention. When he needed water, a change of position, or something else, Bright Star responded immediately. She had done an amazing job setting and splinting his leg, which was broken below the knee but not as badly as I had thought.

That first night was our worst. It was not a cold night, but Buckskin was shivering badly. We put most of our blankets on him. That did not help much. Finally, Bright Star bundled in next to him on one side and put me on the other. Eventually the shaking stopped, and I could tell that the man was asleep. It took a long time for me to go to sleep.

I woke in the morning to the smell of coffee. Sky Hawk brought it to Buckskin and me while Bright Star was making breakfast with a little help from Aspen. While we were waiting, Sky Hawk showed me some branches he had found that he thought could be made into crutches for Buckskin. The boy was very resourceful, and soon Buckskin was hobbling around our camp. He did complain to me that Bright Star hovered over him constantly and would not even let him relieve himself without trying to help. She had not yet spoken to him.

"She has a good heart," I said, "and cares about all human beings even though she is not sure that a white man should be considered among them."

"Well, at least I have been able to get her to turn around and give me some privacy," Buckskin said, as Aspen sat with us.

"Father, what is a nit?" she asked in English.

Buckskin began to look embarrassed.

I looked at him and thought about how to answer. "It is the baby of a bug that I hope you will never know."

"But why did this white man call me a nit at the store?" Aspen persisted.

We were all quiet for a moment, and then Buckskin said, "I am sorry I called you that, little one. I spoke from ignorance." He paused. "No, I spoke from stupidity. I can see that you are kind people who love each other."

Bright Star came to us. "We need to get the stupid one loaded up. We are burning daylight."

We all laughed and prepared to continue our travel. The next few days were uneventful, but our progress was slow. On our fifth day, in the late afternoon, I saw a dust cloud ahead of us and then a group of about four riders coming our way. Telling my family to hide off the trail, I watched until I could see Little Hawk at the front. This was a great relief. As they got closer, Little Hawk broke into a big smile. I motioned for my group to come back.

Little Hawk rode directly to the travois, grunted, then came to me. "I see you have collected another white man. This is becoming a bad habit."

I smiled. "I will tell you about it when we find a place to camp for the night."

The rest of the trip was still slow. It took two more days to reach our village. At one point, Left Alone began to limp. Buckskin found and removed a large thorn from his right rear hoof. From that point on, Left Alone walked directly behind the travois without being led. I was more comfortable now that we had four warriors with us.

Little Hawk and I were able to talk about my trip and about John and Ruth Gale. Their offer was constantly on my mind. My brother asked many questions, mostly about my feelings regarding Maggie, Snow, Storm, and the rest of my family in Dodge City. We talked about my Cheyenne family, which was the village to which we were returning.

It was difficult for me to weigh one against the other. I longed to be with both, but Little Hawk pointed out that it was not possible. His reasoning and ability to think logically amazed me. I was grateful for his advice.

In the end, I decided to return to Maggie and my Dodge City family. Aspen would of course come with me, and I would ask Bright Star to come also. To this day, I believe I made the correct decision, but I continue to miss my Cheyenne family.

Our parting was sad and filled with tears and long hugs. Bright Star did come with us, saying that her place was with me, her son, and her granddaughter who needed her more. It was difficult for her to leave her daughter Blue Sky, Little Hawk, and their children.

It had only been three weeks since Buckskin had broken his leg, but he was doing quite well, and asked if he could come with us to the trading post. He now had a puppy named Little Flea that Aspen had given to him. She traded for it with a song. Left Alone became Buckskin's mule. Wherever Buckskin went, Left Alone was not far behind.

When we were ready to depart, Little Hawk came to me and, with tears, said, "My friend, you have been more of a brother to me than my real brother, whom you killed. I will never forget you, and if we never see each other again in this world, perhaps we will in the next."

I did see Little Hawk again many years later. He did not see me. He was dead.

Miss Goodyear came into the room to check on her patients. "I think that is enough for today. The parents of the little girl Short Feather asked Dr. Cook about are here. Ten-year-old Lydia died before they could get her to surgery, but there was little they could have done. I believe that Short Feather wants to speak with her parents privately. I will take Mr. Ott for a walk."

Charley turned off the tape recorder. Juanita and Grace kissed Short Feather on the forehead, and they all went into the hallway. Snake, on his crutches, followed Miss Goodyear out of the room.

A man and a woman in their late twenties were standing against a wall. They looked tired but stood tall. The man smiled weakly at those coming from the room. The woman did not look up. Lee and Juanita went to them, hugged them, and expressed sincere sorrow for their loss. The others did the same, and Lydia's parents went in to see Short Feather.

Charley and Grace went to get some coffee, as Miss Goodyear walked Snake down the hall. Juanita and Lee wanted to stay.

When Miss Goodyear and Snake returned, Juanita asked, "What happened to Lydia? How did she die?"

"I'm so sorry. You do not know?" asked Miss Goodyear. "It was a drunk driver. It's been in all the papers. She was on her bike when she was hit and dragged almost one hundred feet. God only knows how she lived long enough to get to the hospital."

Both Juanita and Snake needed to sit down. Lee found some chairs. They were all very quiet. Miss Goodyear needed to answer a buzzer.

Twenty minutes later, Lydia's parents came out of the room. They were holding on to each other, and both were smiling. Juanita stood as they stopped in front of her.

"That old man talks with God," said Lydia's father.

Lee said, "Yes, he is a man of prayer."

"I can tell that, but that is not what I mean," Lydia's father spoke with great wonder. "He and God talk to each other. They have conversations. God talks to him."

Lydia's mother spoke through her tears, but still smiling. "He told us things that only Lydia could have told him, even some things that Lydia and I had talked about privately. She called my mother Gran, and Short Feather described my mother perfectly. We now know more than ever that Lydia is with God. I love that old man. He is a miracle."

Lydia's parents walked from the hospital still clinging to each other.

Lee and Juanita looked into the room. Short Feather looked sound asleep, but they could tell he had gone to one of his favorite places. He was smiling.

29

"Dogs and babies are the best judges of character."

—Charley

On Sunday, Lee and Juanita went to church with Charley. Lee was surprised that the service was worshipful but respectful, and "a little low-key." That was the best way he could describe it. Almost everyone there was black and very friendly, welcoming Lee and Juanita with much sincerity and enthusiasm. Juanita loved the service and being with the people. It was the first Protestant evangelical service she had attended.

After church and a light lunch, the three went to Short Feather's apartment. They needed to evaluate how Juanita could stay there and take care of an old man with a broken ankle. The first thing they realized was that the apartment was too small. Short Feather would need to have a hospital-type bed that was adjustable so that he could keep his leg elevated. That was the most comfortable position for him. After looking at the situation from every angle, they became frustrated and decided to go to the hospital.

As they were walking down the hall to Short Feather's room, they passed Dr. Cook going the other way. She stopped and looked at them, saying, "Every time I see that old Indian, I am more amazed. What is he, anyway, some kind of superman?"

None of the three knew how to answer her or what she was talking about. Dr. Cook just shook her head and continued walking down the hall, appearing to be talking to herself.

Dr. Bronson and Edward Conrad were already there when Lee, Juanita, and Charley entered. They were talking quietly, and Short Feather seemed agitated. Snake was not in the room.

Short Feather was saying, "What about Farting Horse? It's not good to leave him here alone. I believe he needs me now more than ever."

"Like you, he is being released tomorrow. They feel he is doing quite well," said Dr. Bronson.

Juanita asked with obvious concern, "What is going on? This old Indian is being sent home after only two days?"

"Dr. Cook just left," said Dr. Bronson.

Lee said, "Yes, we passed her in the hall. She did not seem her usual self."

Dr. Bronson smiled and pointed at the cast on Short Feather's leg. It looked like a patch of plaster had been placed on the inside of the ankle. "Dr. Cook cut an opening in the cast over the incision so that she could check it. She found the incision totally healed, and was quite shocked as was I. After removing the stitches and patching the cast, she just said, 'I don't know why I should have expected anything different. He can go home.' Without saying anything else, she left."

"I am still concerned about Farting Horse," said Short Feather. "He lives by himself and has no one to take care of him. I have come to know him, and he will probably just try to tough it out alone."

Edward took Dr. Bronson by the arm. "We need to find Miss Goodyear and talk about this."

They left and came back about ten minutes later.

Dr. Bronson cleared his throat and began speaking. "Edward and I believe that Short Feather's apartment is too small. Also, we think it is too much for Juanita to try to take care of the patient even with the help of Charley and Grace."

Juanita started to object, but the doctor held up his hand and continued. "Please let me finish. When my mother had surgery,

Allison and I set up our family room so that we could take care of her. There is plenty of room, and there is a full bathroom. We can put in two hospital beds, and Miss Goodyear will come every day for eight hours. We have arranged for her to have leave from the hospital. We will fix up a room for Juanita in my study, which I hardly ever use. If this is agreeable to Snake, he will have the other bed until he is ready to be on his own. This will all cost considerably less than the hospital, and the two patients will have the best care possible. Juanita will be able to work with one of the best nurses I have ever known, gaining much valuable experience."

The room was totally quiet.

Edward finally said, "Well, what do you think?"

Lee spoke up. "I think it is wonderful and very generous of Dr. and Mrs. Bronson."

"To have such wonderful friends is a blessing and a gift from God," said Juanita.

Short Feather looked at Lee and Juanita. "You two need to set a date for your wedding. I am already feeling better, and I do heal quickly." Looking at Edward, he said, "Who is going to tell Farting Horse?"

"Tell me what?" asked Snake as he crutched into the room. He was getting around amazingly well for a man with a cast on one arm and another on his leg.

Edward explained everything, and Snake said with some emotion, "You people are unbelievable."

It was early evening at the Bronson home, and dinner was finished. Juanita was sitting next to Short Feather. Snake appeared to be asleep, with Grace's little schnauzer, Oskar, curled up next to him. Grace was in the kitchen cleaning up. Allison had taken Breeze to a mother/baby group meeting at their church. Dr. Bronson was at the hospital.

"You really scared me, you clumsy old Indian," said Juanita quietly. "I thought we were going to lose you. I don't think any of the doctors or nurses thought you would make it through surgery."

"When it is my time to die, I will go and I will go gratefully," said Short Feather. "It was not my time."

"You are not afraid of dying?"

"Certainly not, my little Buffalo Tail. I will be going to a better place. Far better than anywhere I have ever imagined. If anything, I am excited about embarking on a new adventure. But now, I am not yet ready to go. Jesus understands."

Juanita was thoughtful for a few moments. "Sometimes I have a hard time believing that God is real. There are so many bad things that happen in the world and bad people. Little Lydia being killed by a drunk driver and the Vietnam War are only two examples. Nothing makes sense, and where is God in all of it?"

"Buffalo Tail, as much as I love you and care about you, God is more real to me than you are," Short Feather said. "He is everywhere and everything. All you have to do is open your spirit and look. You must understand, however, that God did not write a book about the world and mankind with everything that has happened and will happen. He is allowing mankind to write the book. He could, of course, intercede, and He has given us the Holy Bible as a guide, but the only thing He has chosen to control totally is the salvation of His children."

"I think I understand most of what you have said."

Short Feather handed Juanita his Bible. "I want you to read the New Testament. When you have questions, come to me, and we will talk about it."

"Can I read it too?" asked Snake. He had been awake and listening.

"Buffalo Tail, please give Farting Horse my Bible," said Short Feather. "I am sure you will find another in your room among Dr. Bronson's books. He will not mind."

"I really want you to stop calling me Farting Horse," said Snake. "I don't like it. You should all just call me Henry."

Short Feather thought for a moment. "I will not call you Farting Horse even though that is your name. I will call you Snake. I do not think I could ever call you Henry."

Oskar jumped down from Snake's bed and went to the front door, wagging his tail and whining. The doorbell rang, and when Grace opened the door, Oskar jumped up on Lee, barking his high-pitched "I'm so glad to see you" bark. Then he did the same to Charley.

"I had to work a little late, and I knew we would miss dinner. Hi, Oskar," said Lee, as he carried in a bag of burgers and fries. Charley was carrying two cups of soft drinks.

Juanita came and kissed Lee in a way that made Grace and Charley look away. It made Lee forget there were others in the room. She kissed Charley on the cheek and said, "It is a lovely evening. Let's go to the patio. I need to get my two men out of bed for a while."

When they were all settled, Lee passed a cheeseburger and a bunch of fries to Charley. There was a considerable amount of fries, and Short Feather said, "Are you going to eat all of those?"

Charley said, "Please help yourself," as he moved his fries closer to Short Feather.

Lee handed a bunch to Snake on a napkin after Juanita and Grace declined. Snake had to guard his from Oskar, who was now sitting on his lap. Grace had already instructed everyone that Oskar was not to have any "people food."

Juanita asked Short Feather, "Grandfather, do you feel up to telling us more of your story?"

"Oh, yes," he said. "As I have told you, it frees my spirit and warms my heart to be able to tell these things to you."

Charley put down his cheeseburger—out of Oskar's reach—and went to get the tape recorder. Juanita fetched the drum.

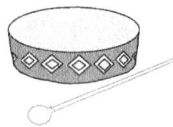

Aspen, Bright Star, Buckskin, and I left our Cheyenne family with heavy hearts. Little Hawk sent his two best warriors, Light Horse and Gray Bull, with us to make sure we got to the trading post safely. It was good of him to do this.

Buckskin was now able to ride his horse, and we made better time even though we had to stop often when his leg began to hurt. Sometimes he would walk for a while using his crutches, with Aspen and the puppy, Little Flea, joyfully running and playing around him. Left Alone was always close behind. Bright Star was keeping watch over all of them. It was a sight to see.

Aspen carefully kept her book with her at all times, the New Testament her "aunt" Ruth had given her at the trading post. Bright Star made a small deerskin bag for her to carry it in. Aspen was persistent at having me read it to her whenever there was time. It was difficult for me because many of the words were strange, and I did not always know their meaning. This is where Buckskin was a big help. He said his father was a traveling preacher, and he had spent many hours, as a boy, listening to sermons. The mountain man was very familiar with the Bible.

On the fourth day, it rained for most of the morning. We did not mind because it kept the dust down and was refreshing. The only problem was that because there was no dust, we had no warning of the troop of mounted Long Knives coming directly at us. We were on the road because in this area, any other route was too dangerous. I think the soldiers were as surprised to see us as we were to see them. We stopped where we were, and so did they, about three hundred paces apart. I counted forty of them, and they had two wagons.

Light Horse and Gray Bull were at the front of our group. Buckskin told them to go to the rear, which they reluctantly did. Buckskin got down from his horse, motioned for me to come, and, using his crutches, started walking to the soldiers. We both left our weapons behind. One of the soldiers, who looked like the officer, started walking to meet us halfway. He brought three soldiers with him, all armed.

When we were close enough to talk, the officer said, "Buckskin, what are you doing way out here with these savages?"

"Lieutenant Davis, it is good to see you," said Buckskin. "I got bucked off my horse and broke my leg. These Injuns found me and saved my life. Their village was wiped out by the coughing sickness. They are the only ones left, and I am taking them to the reservation. They have been good to me."

Lieutenant Davis pointed at me. "This one looks like a Dog Soldier."

I had been looking at the dirt and continued as I put on my dumb look and said, "Ken good Injun."

I recognized one of the three soldiers, and I could tell he recognized me as he said, "Hey, Lieutenant, that is Ken. I remember him from Fort Dodge. Musta been five years ago. Dumb as a rock."

Buckskin looked at me like I was crazy and said to Lieutenant Davis, "We're a day from the trading post, and then we head south. What are you doing out here?"

The officer looked at me again and then at the rest of our group. "We have been ordered to round up the Indians that are scattered all over the foothills. Starting with the closest village about four days from here, then we head north to collect the rest."

"Don't bother with that village," said Buckskin. "It's the one that was wiped out."

Lieutenant Davis looked thoughtful for a few minutes. "Looks like you have them under control. No sense in drag'n 'em with us. Be on your way."

We turned and walked back. I told Gray Bull and Light Horse to look weak and sad as we rode past the soldiers, keeping their weapons hidden under their robes. Bright Star kept Aspen wrapped up in her robe. After about a mile, Light Horse went back to make sure we were not followed. The rest of us waited in a gully.

"That was some act you put on," said Buckskin. "'Ken good Injun,' ha!"

"You did well yourself, Buckskin. Mixing the truth with lies, you almost had me believing you," I said with a smile.

Light Horse returned and said that the Long Knives had moved on. I told him and Gray Bull that they needed to return to the village and warn Little Hawk about the soldiers. Riding fast and hard, they should be there in two days. It was sad to see them go, but I was very concerned.

There were no other incidents, and we arrived at the trading post late in the afternoon the next day. Two large freight wagons and a Conestoga were out front. One of the freight wagons was loaded with skins, furs, and other goods. The other was empty. John and Ruth Gale came out to greet us.

John was smiling. "We are so glad you came. Our usual drivers cannot help us, and Maggie will be so happy to see you."

I introduced Bright Star, and Aspen ran to Ruth to give her a hug. Bright Star looked confused, and I could tell she was uncomfortable. I realized that these were probably the first white people she had ever been near, other than Buckskin, and certainly the first white woman. This was going to be a different world for her, and I needed to be sensitive to that. Ruth looked at me, and I could tell she had observed the same thing.

Ruth saw Buckskin and said, "Buckskin, you are injured. What happened? Oh, dear, where are my manners? You all come inside, and I'll find something cool to drink. I have a stew cooking, and it will be ready in a little bit. You can tell us all about it while we eat."

John and I took care of the animals. The others went inside. Ruth took Bright Star by the arm and Aspen by the hand, leading them in. Buckskin followed close behind on his crutches with his puppy, Little Flea. Ruth and John did not seem to mind.

Ruth and Bright Star made some wonderful biscuits to go with the stew. Over dinner, Buckskin told about his encounter with the mountain lion and how I had saved his life. He praised Bright Star for how she had taken care of him, never mentioning that she hovered and pestered him. Holding Little Flea, he told how Aspen had traded a song for the puppy.

Ruth insisted that Aspen sing the song for us, which she did in Cheyenne. I translated.

> My mother is with the Great Spirit
> She watches over me
> I know she loves me still
> My father helps me see her face.
> When I am grown and know my way
> I want to smile and laugh and love
> Just like my mother, who is with the Great Spirit.

There was not a dry eye in the room.

Short Feather stopped drumming and opened his eyes.

Everyone was emotional, including Allison, who was standing at the door holding her baby, Breeze.

30

"Good intentions can be very dangerous."

—Short Feather

The next morning, Juanita was up early to prepare breakfast and plan the day. Part of her responsibility was to see that Short Feather and Snake got some exercise. Snake did better than Short Feather, except she really had to badger him to do the leg lifts sitting in a chair. But Snake did them and then decided to take a walk around the yard. Short Feather refused to do the chair exercises until Juanita threatened to leave.

"You need to do your exercises if you are going to walk me down the aisle, you stubborn old Indian," said Juanita heatedly. "Are all old people this exasperating?"

Short Feather smiled. "I'm old, tired, and exercise hurts. Besides, all the exercise in the world won't make me any younger."

"No, but it could make you stronger and less wobbly. I don't want to have to hold you up walking down the aisle if you live that long."

"Don't get your hopes up, squirt, I'll be there. Have you and Lee set a date yet?"

"We have decided on July 23. It is only a few weeks away in case you decided to leave us." Juanita became serious and asked quietly, "Grandfather, how long do you expect... *want* to live?"

"I do not know how long I will live, but I do know how I will die," Short Feather said. "I will simply go to one of my better places and not come back. But I want to finish my story and see that you are properly married. Ultimately, however, I am leaving it all up to God."

"I am reading the New Testament," said Juanita. "And I always pray that God will help me understand. It is beautiful, and although I have read parts before, it is like I am reading it for the first time. I love the Sermon on the Mount in Matthew 5. I've read it four or five times."

"Yes, it is one of my favorite passages also," said Short Feather.

At 8:00 a.m., Miss Goodyear arrived. She asked that now she should be called by her first name, Jane, but Short Feather gave her an Indian name, Sunshine Woman. Snake's insurance company agreed to pay for half of the nursing care and also compensation to the Bronsons for room and board. They were getting off easy, and knew it.

Juanita, however, was not covered, so Snake put her on his company's payroll as a temporary executive assistant. They set it up to deposit the money into her savings account since she had few expenses.

Sunshine Woman—Miss Goodyear—brought in the medications and asked how things were going.

"This old Indian refused to do his exercises until I threatened him," said Juanita. "Snake has gone outside."

"Short Feather, you must do what you are told," said Sunshine Woman. "The doctors know best, and it is all in their instructions."

Short Feather scrunched up his face, trying to look angry. "Women, you gang up on us men. What pills are you giving me? Are they a narcotic?"

"Yes, they are the painkillers that Dr. Cook prescribed for you," said the nurse.

Short Feather looked at the pills. "Do I have to take them? I don't like what they do to me."

The nurse got the instruction sheet that Dr. Cook sent and read it again. "The doctor does say that you should take them 'as needed,' but you will have more pain if you stop."

"I'll take the pain in my leg any day over the pain in my head. I'll just take aspirin or that new stuff that is supposed to work. I think it is called Tylenol."

"Edward is coming by later," said Sunshine Woman. "He can pick some up on the way."

Short Feather chuckled. "Edward, is it? He comes by every day, but I know it is not to see me. Tornado only comes to see you, Sunshine Woman, and the baby, Breeze."

Sunshine Woman gave a sly smile and left to call Edward's secretary.

By 10:30 a.m., both men were bathed and shaved, soaking up the beautiful day on the patio. Edward was holding Breeze and flirting with Sunshine Woman. They both loved the name Short Feather had given her. Juanita was reading the book of John from the New Testament to Short Feather and Snake. Snake stopped her often to ask questions or make comments. Edward had brought Grace and Oskar with him. Grace was in the kitchen, and Oskar was curled up next to Snake again. This had become Oskar's favorite place to be.

After lunch, Edward had to leave for a court appearance. Snake spent the afternoon dealing with his office. He had a second phone line installed so that he did not tie up the Bronsons' phone. Juanita and Sunshine Woman took care of housekeeping chores, and Short Feather took a nap—a long nap—most of the afternoon.

Juanita and Sunshine Woman talked as they worked.

"I think that Short Feather is getting weaker, not stronger," said Juanita.

Sunshine Woman looked concerned. "Broken bones and surgery can be hard on a person at any age. You need to remember that he is one hundred and ten years old. Some would say it is a miracle that he has lived this long."

"Yes," said Juanita. "I am grateful that I have known Grandfather as long as I have. Whatever time I have left with him, I will consider a gift from God."

Two days later, everyone was together in the evening. The Bronsons had been able to listen to the tape and catch up with Short Feather's story.

Short Feather was feeling better, having stopped taking the painkillers. Picking up his drum and closing his eyes, he continued his story.

A few days after we arrived at the Gales' store, we were all ready to head for Dodge City. Buckskin decided to come with us. He was able to drive the third wagon, which he said was much easier on his leg than riding a horse.

I put on my white-man clothes, and Ruth dressed Bright Star and Aspen in calico dresses and bonnets. Everyone agreed that this was a good thing to do in case we were seen and questioned by Long Knives. I kept all my weapons hidden but within easy reach.

The trip took three days, and the evenings around the campfire were filled with storytelling and reading the New Testament. Sometimes we sang songs. It reminded me of my family and our time together in the mountains before Mother and Father were killed at Washita. My memories of Peppermint and my need to find her were always on my mind. I will forever be grateful to John and Ruth. They treated us kindly and with respect. Buckskin had become part of our family.

"Grandfather, I have a question." Juanita interrupted quietly.

Short Feather stopped drumming and opened his eyes. "Yes, my little Buffalo Tail, what is it?"

"I remember that you said Buckskin was not a big man, but how old was he, and what did he look like?"

"When we first saw him, he had long reddish-brown hair and a beard. A full beard, so we did not really know his face. But he did have very blue eyes that seemed to sparkle when he smiled. While in the Cheyenne village, he decided to shave off his beard, but after cutting himself several times, Bright Star took over and did a beautiful job without a nick. Buckskin turned out to be quite handsome, and was probably thirty-five years old, a few years older than Bright Star."

Lee asked, "Grandfather, it sounds like Bright Star and Buckskin were becoming close. Did they have a relationship?"

"Yes, they did," answered Short Feather. "I don't want to get ahead of my story, but they did marry. Bright Star was very young, about fourteen, when she and Willow's father, Son of the Wind, married. He was much older, almost forty. He married her mainly to take care of his home, but he treated her well. Bright Star had great respect for Son of the Wind but told me once that she never really loved him as a husband. He was more of a father figure to her. Her second marriage to Buckskin was totally different. They clearly loved and respected each other, and as a bonus, they were best friends."

"Now I must continue my story." Short Feather closed his eyes and began drumming again.

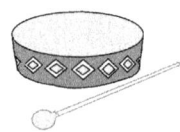

John Gale stopped his wagon right in front of Maggie's and Snow's mercantile store in Dodge City.

Almost before my feet touched the ground, both Maggie and Snow had me wrapped in their arms. We all had tears. Then Sage Woman hugged me, and Storm almost squeezed the air out of me with his one arm. Standing back a little were Sunrise, Snow's daughter—who was now thirteen—and eighteen-year-old Rain Catcher, Sage Woman's son by her first marriage. Both looked wonderful, although a little shy. When I opened my arms to them, they both ran to me with big smiles.

Aspen was standing off to the side with Bright Star and Ruth Gale. I took her hand and introduced my daughter to my Dodge City family. She smiled and took to them right away, greeting and hugging each of them, just like her mother would have done. It was hard for me to see so much of Willow in her, but I would not have wanted her to be anything different.

After introducing Bright Star and Buckskin, I noticed that there was a white man standing at the door of the store with a big friendly smile. He was very well-dressed, as was all of my family. He looked familiar, but I could not place him in my memory.

Storm saw that I was looking at the man and took me to meet him. "Short Feather, this is William Ward."

The man held out his hand for me to shake.

"He is my business partner and adviser, the man from the East who bought our merchandise so many years ago," Storm went on. "You should also know that he is Maggie's husband as of last year."

Maggie came and took William's arm, smiling brightly at me. She was holding Aspen. I could tell by the look on her face that she loved William very much, and his look toward her said that he loved her.

"Maggie has told me all about you and how you met," said William. "I know that we are going to be great friends."

His handshake was warm and firm. The look in his eyes and his bearing unsettled me. Other than Willow, I had never felt such love coming from a human being, and he…was a white man.

Allison put her hand to her mouth and gasped, looking at her husband.

Short Feather stopped drumming and opened his eyes.

Allison asked, "Did you say his name was William Ward, from the East?"

Short Feather smiled. "It has been hard for me to wait until now to tell this part of my story. Yes, his name was William Ward III, and he was from a small town in Connecticut called Owenstown. He was raised in a close and loving family. A black woman named Nanalee Bronson was his nanny, although she was much more than that."

Dr. Jacob Bronson spoke softly, and with wonder. "This is amazing. What a small world we live in. My great-great-grandfather changed his slave name to Bronson because Nanalee Bronson had such a great impact on his life as a boy. Years after her death, he found out that she had financed his education. She was a very wealthy black woman, but few ever knew that."

Juanita and the rest were amazed. She asked, "What was William Ward like?"

"He was not a big or imposing man, about five feet nine inches tall. I would not call him handsome but pleasant, kind, and calm looking." Short Feather went on. "In 1879, he was thirty-three years old and a very successful entrepreneur and investor. He purchased some land in California, where he intended to grow seedless grapes for raisins. All of my Dodge City family decided to move there with Maggie and William. Aspen and I went with them."

"Whoa," said Lee. "Aren't you getting ahead of yourself and skipping some things? When did you realize the connection between Dr. Bronson and William Ward?"

"It was at the park by the lake when we first met the Bronsons and Snake," answered Short Feather. "Somehow I knew we would all become good friends. But now I must continue my story."

The next few days were very busy. My Cheyenne family and my Dodge City family came together as one. Aspen was full of joy all of the time, except when she fell off the pony Rain Catcher was training for her. He trained one for Sunrise to be gentle and easy to ride. Aspen and her pony still had much to learn, but when she fell and scrapped her knee, she got right back on, just like her mother would have. The rest of the family was preparing to move to California.

The store and bathhouse were offered to John and Ruth Gale to run. They were ecstatic about the opportunity to move to town, only concerned about who would run their trading post.

Bright Star found that she was missing her daughter, Blue Sky, Little Hawk, and her grandchildren more than she ever expected, even though she was much attached to me and Aspen. She did not want to move so far away. Buckskin was reluctant to leave also since he loved the open plains.

Buckskin requested my permission to ask Bright Star to marry him.

William Ward and Maggie worked everything out. They would trade 90 percent of the Dodge City businesses to the Gales for the trading post and everything that went with it. Buckskin and Bright Star would run the trading post with help from the Gales.

Bright Star decided she needed a white-woman name. Maggie suggested Bridget, which is a Celtic name meaning "strong." Bright Star, now Bridget, was very pragmatic, much like Storm. She was able to assimilate and change depending on the circumstances in which she found herself. I did not change so easily.

Thunderstorm, his wife, Sage Woman, and his sister, Snow Flower, were now doing well financially, thanks to their own initiative and association with Maggie and William Ward. They made good money making Indian clothing, mainly moccasins, and also white Western men's and women's clothing. William was a genius at investing, and had been able to multiply their savings. I also found out that they had always considered me to be a part of their enterprises and had set aside a substantial fund for me.

It took another three weeks to ready ourselves to move to California and transfer control of the businesses to the Gales and the new Mr. and Mrs. Gregory. In July of 1879, we had everything loaded on a train and left for our new home.

Breeze began to fuss a little, and Oskar jumped from Snake's lap to see what was wrong. Allison took Breeze to change her diapers. Oskar walked into the yard to do what dogs do.

Short Feather stretched and seemed to be in some pain, although he said nothing.

"Are you all right, Grandfather?" asked Juanita.

Short Feather flexed the arm and hand with which he had been tapping the drum. "My arm is stiff, and my hand is cramped a little. Perhaps it would be better if you played my drum while I continue my story, Buffalo Tail."

Dr. Bronson came and massaged the arm and hand. "It might be best if we stop and let you rest. We can continue on another day."

"No, I would like to go on. There are things I want to tell you that are important," said Short Feather, as he closed his eyes. "I will just rest quietly until Allison returns."

Juanita looked at Dr. Bronson, who smiled and gave an affirmative nod. They were both concerned because Short Feather looked tired.

When Allison returned, Short Feather opened his eyes and motioned to Juanita. She started drumming, and he closed his eyes.

We worked very hard the first two years in California. There were houses to build and vineyards to plant. Rain Catcher took care of our cattle, horses, and other farm animals with the help of some hired hands. He was very good at this, and everyone called him Catch. Storm was amazing in that he was able to do more with one arm than most men could do with two. Snow and Sunrise opened a clothing store in the growing town of Los Angeles. They lived in rooms above the store. Maggie was a part owner. Since we were there often and it was about thirty miles from our ranch, William, Storm, and I built a house near the store.

Maggie opened a school because she loved children and teaching. Aspen learned quickly and always had a book with her to read. The days were full. I always went to bed tired but never failed to tell Aspen about her mother. She never seemed to tire of this even though I had told the same stories many times. I also told her about my sister, Peppermint, who was on my mind constantly, along with an ache in my heart.

William, Storm, and I had many long and important talks about life and responsibilities. We talked about everything, from religion, politics, and economics to ranching and growing grapes for raisins. They were both followers of Jesus but never put pressure on me. Even though I had been reading the Bible and was impressed with the teachings, I still struggled with the fact that it was the white man's religion and white men had all but obliterated my people. It pained me to hear about Indian reservations and what was happening.

After four years, with things settling down, Storm and William suggested that I travel to some of the reservations to see for myself and see if we could help. I welcomed the opportunity and decided to take Aspen with me. The first thing we did, however, was go to visit Buckskin and Bright Star, now Stephen and Bridget.

The trading post had been doing well. Because of their loving and caring natures, Stephen and Bridget were accepted into the community of surrounding farms and ranches. With the nearest doctor over fifty miles away, Bridget looked to the medical needs of the community and was well-loved and honored. She delivered many babies and had more than one little girl named after her.

Little Hawk, Blue Sky, and their children were able to visit the trading post often, much to the delight of Bridget. Indians of different tribes often came to Stephen and Bridget for help. Life was difficult for the Indians, and most were being moved to reservations, where surviving was even more difficult.

Aspen asked if she could stay at the trading post with her grandmother when I left to visit the reservations. My daughter was happy and excited to be with Buckskin, Little Flea, and Left Alone (the mule), who had become a family pet. He was also a main attraction at the trading post, always happy to give rides to children.

It was good that I left Aspen with her grandmother. She was only seven years old, and what I saw at the reservations was hard and distressed me greatly. I will not dwell on the conditions I found. All has been well-documented. Suffice it to say that what I saw was horrible at best and that it is amazing that anyone survived. The causes of the terrible conditions were numerous. Greed, ambition, bigotry, pride, and alcoholism were among the worst. Like many others, I tried to fight and work against these, but failures were many and successes were few.

By far, the worst cause of the plight of my people and the one that was impossible to defeat was the "good intentions" of government and religion. I have come to despise "good intentions." While I fear few things, I very much fear "good intentions" and their inevitable consequences.

As an example, white Christian missionaries opened schools to educate Indian children—good people with good intentions. The parents of the children did not want them educated in the white culture. Fearing that Indian culture would be destroyed, they did not send them to the schools. The good people with good intentions and the help of government took the children from their parents. Only English was taught and allowed to be spoken at the schools.

Once, I came upon a white man savagely beating a small Arapaho boy. I stopped him and asked why he was beating the child. He said the child had spoken Indian words in class. I was then arrested, and spent three nights in jail. No charges were ever filed against me or the white man.

Short Feather stopped. He seemed to be struggling with his words.

"Are you all right, Grandfather?" asked a concerned Juanita.

"Yes, I am fine," he said. "It has just been so hard for me to see the way my people were treated. I wish I could have done more to help. So many of us tried only to see things get worse. The destruction of the Native American culture was mainly accomplished with good intentions. I look at what is happening too many of our communities in this country: white, black, Mexican, Indian. They are being decimated by well-meaning people who are not considering the consequences of their good deeds. The riot in Watts, just last year, is an example of what I am talking about. I cannot say that welfare is the cause of all of the problems, but at best, it has certainly not helped."

Dr. Bronson agreed. "I once heard our pastor say about our black communities that 'welfare is a self-perpetuating degradation, the worst thing that ever happened to my people.' And yes, it all started with good intentions of well-meaning people."

Short Feather sighed. "I spent the next ten years and indeed many years after trying to help my people. With many nights in jail and more than a few attempts on my life, I spoke to large groups, families, and individuals. Eventually I spoke in churches, as Storm did. Aspen was almost always with me. People loved her and were drawn to her. She was always smiling and talking about Jesus."

Usually, Charley was quiet unless someone spoke to him, but he spoke now. "Grandfather, you have never told us what caused you to believe in Jesus. We know that you saw many negatives in those who claimed to follow Him and you avoid using the word *Christian*."

"It was a long process," replied Short Feather.

Snake, with Oskar back on his lap, paid close attention.

"God used many people and things to bring me to Himself," Short Feather went on. "The turning point came when I met a man who followed Jesus but refused to call himself a Christian. He was a Jewish man. He said that most Jews do not trust people who call themselves Christians and that all we have to do is look at history to see why. He believed in Jesus when he was able to separate the Man and His teachings from mankind. We talked for many hours.

"God used another man to influence me: Judas. Here was a man that lived with, ate with, worked with Jesus, the greatest teacher and philosopher of all time. And yet he betrayed Him. I believe that Colonel Chivington betrayed Jesus at Sand Creek, and the missionary that beat the little Arapaho boy also betrayed Him. It is not logical to judge a man based on the actions of those who betray him. I was able to see Jesus as an individual, as God sees us, and separate Him from the actions of those who claim to follow Him. When I did this, it was only a few small steps to accept Him as the Son of God and my Savior. Also, reading the New Testament to Aspen opened my eyes to many truths."

"Grandfather, you look very tired. Perhaps we should stop now," said a concerned Juanita.

"Please," said Short Feather. "There is one more memory that I would like to tell you. It is very special to me, and I would like to play the drum while I tell it."

Juanita gave him the drum. He closed his eyes and began beating a soft steady rhythm.

Thump, thump, thump, thump.

Speaking softly yet clearly, Short Feather went on with his story.

I continued to tell Aspen about her mother, my beautiful Willow, whenever we were together, usually before bedtime. She never seemed to tire of my stories, and I grew to love telling her even though I still had an ache in my heart.

One night, when Aspen was twelve years old, I told her again how her mother was always happy and how she loved helping and caring for others. When I finished, she became very quiet and said, "Father, tell me again what my mother looked like."

I looked at my daughter, and found it hard to speak. I finally said, "My dear sweet daughter, go to the mirror, and you will see your mother's face."

Aspen went to the mirror and began to cry. We cried together for a very long time.

The drumbeat changed.

Thump-thump, thump-thump, thump-thump, thump-thump.

Short Feather's eyes remained closed. His breathing was quiet, but the drumbeat went on.

Juanita became frightened and looked to Dr. Bronson.

The doctor came and checked Short Feather's pulse. "He is okay, Juanita. I think he has gone to one of his favorite places. The drumbeat matches his heartbeat perfectly."

This went on for another twenty minutes. Finally, Short Feather opened his eyes and said, "Buffalo Tail, please help me to my bed."

31

"Simple pleasures can brighten our lives."

—Short Feather

The next few days were quiet and restful. Short Feather and Snake talked for many hours, always finding time to take a break for a nap. Juanita made sure that both men did their exercises. Snake kept getting stronger. Short Feather struggled and did not have much of an appetite, eating little.

Early Saturday morning, a loud motorcycle with a sidecar pulled into the driveway. Hugo—Hugh Westgate—came to the door. Juanita let him in and took him to the patio, where Snake and Short Feather were soaking up the sunshine and drinking coffee.

"Well, look at you two good-for-nothing lazy bums," Hugo said with a laugh. "What a life you have with this beautiful young lady here to wait on you."

Snake reached out to shake Hugo's hand. "It is good to see you. What are you doing here? You should be out riding, it is a great day."

"I came to see if you wanted to go for a ride with me."

Snake looked disappointed. "There is no way I could ride a bike with my arm and leg still in casts."

"Could you get into a sidecar?" Hugo asked. "I had one put on my bike just for you and your buddy here if he would like to go next."

"A sidecar," said Snake excitedly. "I know I could do that."

"Me too," said Short Feather.

"No way," exclaimed Juanita. "Not while I am in charge. If Snake wants to kill himself, that's one thing, but you have to be in my wedding, you stupid old man."

Allison heard everything and agreed with Juanita.

Snake was able to get into the sidecar with a little help from Hugo, and they took off down the road. Short Feather watched wistfully from his wheelchair as they left.

"It has been many years since I have ridden a motorcycle. I would really like to go, and if Snake can get into the sidecar, so can I," he said forcefully. "I will take Hugo up on his offer, and that is final. I have made it this far, and I don't think a short ride will hurt me."

Juanita turned and walked back into the house, leaving Short Feather to get himself back in.

An hour and a half later, Hugo and Snake returned. Snake was smiling like a little kid. Short Feather wheeled himself back out and was lifted into the sidecar by Hugo. Juanita and Allison came out and stood next to Snake on his crutches. Hugo gunned the bike and took off down the road.

Over the roar of the engine, everyone could hear Short Feather yelling like a "wild Indian."

Juanita paced until the return of the happy bikers an hour later. She gave Hugo a dirty look, but when she saw the joy on Short Feather's face, she gave Hugo a hug. Short Feather wanted to know what was for lunch. He said he was starving.

Bending to hug Short Feather as he sat in his wheelchair, Juanita whispered in his ear, "It's not even eleven thirty yet, you old Indian. I was worried sick."

About that time, Lee pulled up with Charley, Grace, and Oskar. Lee walked over to the sidecar and said, "Wow, that looks great. Are you giving rides?"

"Forget it," said Juanita, as she took him by the hand and dragged him into the house.

Everyone laughed.

Lee announced that he was going to take Juanita out for lunch and a drive to the beach. Everyone agreed that it was a great idea and her men would be just fine since Sunshine Woman was there. Juanita had been taking care of Short Feather and Snake for over a week.

Allison and Grace fixed a great lunch. Short Feather ate more than he had in days and sat back in his favorite chair on the patio, holding Breeze. Oskar jumped up with them, and soon, all three were sound asleep, with Breeze drooling a little on Short Feather's chest. Allison quietly took pictures.

Around 3:00 p.m., Rudy and Sara Drake stopped by to visit Short Feather. Rudy was the friend who had introduced Lee to Short Feather weeks before. They had a nice visit, and Sara was amazed at the friendships, not to mention an engagement, that were established because of that one introduction. When Lee and Juanita returned, they all visited for a while longer until the Drakes had to leave.

After dinner, Short Feather wanted to tell more of his story. Picking up the drum and closing his eyes, he continued.

The next years were spent working at our ranch, visiting reservations, and still trying to find out something about my sister, Peppermint. I was beginning to lose any hope that I would ever see her again.

In the spring of 1888, I was reading the newspaper in the kitchen of our home in Los Angeles and saw an advertisement that caught my attention with a jolt. It said the following:

Lyceum Theatre
June 8, 9, 10
Three nights only!
Julia Pepper Cornelius

Just back from her celebrated tour of Europe including a command performance before Queen Victoria, Pepper will sing all your favorite songs. This is a concert not to be missed. Limited seating, get your tickets early.

This was just too much of a coincidence, and it had been almost twenty years since Peppermint had been taken by the Long Knives. I rushed to the theater and bought three tickets: one for myself, one for Maggie, and one for Aspen. The only night available was the tenth, Sunday, and the only seats available were near the back.

Maggie and I tried to find out when and where the singer would be arriving, but we were unable to get any information. I did look through the papers and found an article about Pepper Cornelius in the entertainment section. It indicated she was quite a celebrity in the East and we were very fortunate to have such a talented entertainer in our city.

On the evening of June 10, 1888, I dressed in my finest clothes. I even shined my shoes. If this woman was not my sister, at least I could enjoy the concert and not feel too uncomfortable. Maggie wore her best dress, and Aspen, now twelve years old, was beautiful in her new dress that Maggie and Snow had helped her pick out. In spite of my white-man clothes, I still looked like an Indian, with sharp facial features, dark copper skin tone, and long hair with my feather. But, as Snow said, I cleaned up good, and they should let me in.

They did let me in, although I got some strange looks. It seemed like every high-class person from the city and surrounding area was there. The mayor and his wife were among the last to be seated, and of course, they sat in the front. We heard that they had been at the Friday concert, so this was their second. I was uncomfortable and nervous, but with Maggie on one side and Aspen on the other, I was able to calm down. They each took and held one of my hands. Aspen told me to stop bouncing my knee.

We sat for what seemed a long time until a man dressed in a tuxedo walked out on the stage and asked everyone to rise. The curtain opened, revealing a small orchestra that began to play the national anthem. Everyone stood and put their hand over their heart and sang. I stood but did not sing. Only Maggie and Aspen noticed.

The man came out again and gave a short speech about Julia Pepper Cornelius and her illustrious career. Then he said, "It is my honor to introduce to you the songbird of the East, Julia Pepper Cornelius."

My heart almost stopped when a woman who looked exactly like my mother walked out on the stage. She was absolutely beautiful in a soft dark-blue satin gown, with her hair done up in the latest fashion. Even from way in the back, I could see her eyes sparkle. Both Maggie and Aspen had to ask me to let go of their hands since I was crushing them.

"She is Peppermint, is she not?" asked Maggie, as she blotted her tears.

"Yes, there is no doubt," I answered.

Peppermint stood smiling in front of the orchestra until the applause stopped and the room became quiet. Nodding to the conductor, the orchestra played a prelude to "Amazing Grace," and then Peppermint began to sing. With a strong and clear voice, she sang all the verses. I had never heard anyone sing as well as she, and there was a standing ovation when she finished the hymn.

She went on to sing many of the popular songs of the day, and then she sang a very moving rendition of "Oh Shenandoah." Peppermint made an already beautiful song even more beautiful, and it became one of my favorites.

Near the end of the concert, she sang an emotional version of "Dixie," and many men stood with tears streaming down their faces. Then Peppermint started an equally emotional version of "The Battle Hymn of the Republic." In the middle of the last chorus, I stood and moved to the center aisle. Walking halfway to the stage, I stopped when she saw me. She stopped singing, and a few bars later, the orchestra stopped. There were questioning murmurs in the audience. Peppermint looked at me for almost a full minute and then began to smile.

With her eyes still on me, Peppermint removed some pins and a comb from her hair, and it fell black and shiny over her shoulders. Taking a handkerchief from her sleeve, she wiped the theatrical makeup from her face. Now she looked more like a Cheyenne, and she began to sing, in Cheyenne, her song from so long ago:

> The sun rises and the dark runs away,
> I rejoice and welcome a new day.

> The earth is warm
> The sky is clear
> I have no worry
> My family is near.

> A stream of clear water flows from the hill
> It quenches my thirst and the sound keeps me still.

> The earth is warm
> The sky is clear
> I have no worry
> My family is near.

> This is my home in this valley of love
> I will always remember this gift from above.

The earth is warm
The sky is clear
I have no worry
My family is near.

As she sang, she walked off the stage and down the stairs. A gentleman in the front gave her his hand to help her on the stairs. As she walked slowly toward me, there was more murmuring from the audience, but she did not notice. When she got to me, she stopped and was looking directly into my eyes with a wonderful smile.

Grabbing my coat and pulling me toward her, she said with a shaky voice, "My brother, why did it take you so long to find me?"

I could think of nothing to say and was unable to speak.

Jumping a little, she put her arms around my neck, and I held her for a very long time. We were both crying.

Then she said, "Please, take me home, Short Feather," and we left, with Maggie and Aspen close behind.

Juanita, Allison, and Grace were crying quietly. No one made a sound, and the drumming stopped. Snake tried unsuccessfully to wipe away the tears that were falling from his eyes while rubbing Oskar's head at the same time.

After a while, Lee spoke. "Grandfather, can you tell us more? That is certainly not the end of your story."

"There is much more to tell," said Short Feather. "But it will have to be at another time. I am very tired. This has been a wonderful and busy day."

32

"If you know the ending, it is over. I prefer to dream on."

—The Author

Juanita went in to see Short Feather the next morning. It was Sunday. She found him sound asleep, and decided to let him sleep in. He seemed so peaceful, and his breathing was shallow and quiet. Snake had already gotten up and was in the kitchen getting coffee. Juanita sat by Short Feather's bed and watched his face, marveling at the life he had led. She noticed that his hand was moving like he was tapping his drum, but there was no drum.

After a while, Juanita decided it was time to wake him. Kissing him gently on the forehead, she shook his shoulder. There was no response.

"Grandfather, you need to wake up," she said.

There was no response, and it seemed like he was not breathing.

Beginning to panic, Juanita said loudly, "Don't you do this to me, you selfish old Indian. I need you and love you so much!"

Nothing.

Allison and Snake heard Juanita, and came in quickly, followed by Dr. Bronson. The doctor listened to Short Feather's heart and breathing.

"His heart sounds good. His breathing is shallow," said the doctor. "It is almost like he is in a trance and not responding to his surroundings. All we can do is wait for him to come out of it. How long has his hand been moving like that? It's like he is playing his drum."

"I noticed it a few minutes ago," said Juanita. "He isn't dying, is he? He told me he would just go to a better place and not come back."

"I see no sign that his body is in distress. If anything, he is super calm and relaxed," said the doctor. "I am amazed that he is able to do this."

Juanita stayed by Short Feather as the others left the room. She put her hand on his, but the drumming without a drum continued. After about an hour, Juanita was sound asleep, sitting in her chair with her arms and head on the bed. She awoke suddenly as Lee walked into the room. Jumping up, she went to him, and they hugged. Lee was looking at Short Feather, who had not moved except for his hand.

Lee said quietly, "He looks so peaceful and calm. Snake told me what was going on."

"Oh, Lee, I am so glad you are here. I don't want to lose him. Please tell me he will be okay."

Lee said with sincerity, "Dr. Bronson says that physically he is doing well. I believe he will come back to us."

Lee and Juanita sat by the bed for another hour, and then Juanita started to cry again.

"Why are you crying, Buffalo Tail?" said Short Feather. "I need to tell you Peppermint's story and about my grandchildren."

Lee smiled, handed the drum to Short Feather, and turned on the tape recorder. Juanita laughed and cried at the same time.

Short Feather closed his eyes and began tapping the drum.

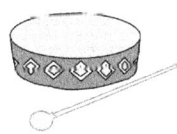

After leaving the Lyceum Theater, we walked toward home. Two very large men followed close behind. Peppermint said they were her bodyguards, and…

Thump thump thump.

Note to the Reader

Yes, I know, there are many unanswered questions. What is Peppermint's story? What happened to Maggie, William, and Storm, just to name a few? Whom did Aspen marry? Was Short Feather at Juanita and Lee's wedding? What about Snake?

As one reader said, "I just can't wait to find out what happens next."

My answer is, "Me too."

If you have any ideas or comments, please let me know. Maybe there will be another book.

As an author, the simplest thing for me to do would have been to have Short Feather die in the end. I could not do that, however, because I promised my wife, Joyce, and my granddaughter, Jane, that that would not happen. And a promise is a promise.

Thank you for reading.

—Larry

CPSIA information can be obtained
at www.ICGtesting.com
Printed in the USA
FSOW03n0656110916
24843FS